A Kayak
for One

Book one in the six book Kirk Lake Camp series.

K.L. MCCLUSKEY

Cover by: Arthur McBain

An Taigh Buidhe air an Lohan Publishing

ISBN:9781775236184

DEDICATION

This book is dedicated to my mother,

Rose McCluskey

(September 19th, 1931-September 24th, 2015)

ACKNOWLEDGMENTS

I would like to be able to thank my mother for her encouragement in getting me started on A Kayak for One, my first book. Her enthusiasm and belief that I would serve myself better if I wrote down the words that were piling up in my head, motivated me to just get at it. Sadly, my mother died before I completed the book.

My thanks and appreciation go out to Arthur, my partner, who listened to my idea for a series of books and told me he thought it was a great idea. His continued support and encouragement have helped guide me through my writing. We have shared our thoughts about the characters and had lots of laughs over zany ideas for the plots in the six book Kirk Lake Camp series set in northern Ontario.

I would like to thank Arthur for all his work at getting my book formatted properly, as well as acknowledge his creativity and artistry in designing the cover for the book.

Last, but not least, I would like to thank my family members and friends who read this book in its rough stages and asked me when book two would be finished.

CHAPTER 1

Tuesday September 22nd, 2015

Charlie

Charlie looked up and out the bedroom window at the morning sky and maple branches just as the loon started its call. Just hearing the plaintive, haunted cry made getting up out of bed to look out through the tree branches toward the lake worthwhile, that, and the autumnal reds and oranges of the maple leaves on the branches that almost touched the second-floor bedroom window. The birches along the shoreline were still bright yellow. Though the tamarack was still holding onto its green hue, Charlie knew the hard season was almost over.

It was 7:05 am. The alarm clock was set for 7:20 so Charlie made sure to turn it off, not wanting to hear the jarring sound if not needed. There had been too many years of early alarm get-ups with the variety of bells, beeps, buzzes and noises that came from the alarm clock, radio alarms, pagers, and now the cell phone. That done, Charlie padded out naked to the kitchen and turned the coffee on, then moved to the living room to nudge the thermostat of the propane fireplace up to some respectful temperature, then moved next into the bathroom. Having learned from experience with the season change and dark early mornings, Charlie looked first to make sure the shutters were tightly closed on the big window over the tub before turning on the light. Now near the end of September the sun was still just rising. After a quick wash and listen to see whether it was time to go turn down the stove element under the percolator, it was time to get dressed for work, starting with long underwear bottoms and top, thick wool socks, wind pants, and a flannel shirt. The hot shower would come at the end of the day. There was no point at the start.

Charlie slipped on a well-worn pair of moose-skin moccasins, thinking, not for the first time, that it was time to buy another pair. They had been re-stitched with heavy thread last year, but that wouldn't work again, and the thick-skin soles were no longer thick all over. It would be tough to find some with the padded bottoms. The trading posts in the area seem to be stocking more moccasins with a designer look and less substance, rather than those made for everyday wear, for going in and out of the house, at least on dry days. The shopping trip though, like anything else personal, would have to wait.

With fresh coffee in the thermos, Charlie started down the stairs. Breakfast would come after the coffee, making the most of the strong black coffee first.

CHAPTER 2

Bob

He woke up where he fell asleep. It wasn't the first time and wouldn't be the last that it wouldn't be his bed. He dug the heels of his hands into his eyes and rubbed the Jim Beam and sleep from them. He shoved the chesterfield cushions aside, rolled up to sit, and looked out the wall-to-wall windows across the lake. He smiled. The lights in the office were on at the resort across the narrow channel of water. Charlie was up. He reached for the binoculars.

CHAPTER 3

Dan

"Fuck. I am fucked."

There was no point keeping this as an inside-the-head phrase. It only felt better saying it out loud, but not so loud to disturb anyone. Who would hear anyway? Charlie? Looking out the window over the bed toward the house, Dan could see the light in the bathroom, just showing between the thin spaces between the slats of the shutter. Charlie must be up then. The students would be asleep though. They had youth on their side and the late beer nights after studying would allow them to sleep soundly. He better be careful though. The resort was dead quiet, with only the loon and nuthatches making any noise this early. There were other cottages on the lake but spaced out well and tucked in to the trees. Unlike a lot of the recreation lakes in northern Ontario, around here there were only a handful of cottages and they each had lots of acreage. Most were built by Americans in the 1950s and many third generation family members came to the lake for just a few weeks in the summer, happy to use what their

4

grandparents paid for, decades before them.

The six hour drive from Toronto kept a lot of people away. That, and there was no road to most of the cottages. The resort wasn't on an island as most people thought when Dan described the area to them, but most of the land was provincial park and a First Nation reserve. The dirt road in to the back half of the land was on reserve land, for reserve use only, and there was no road access into the park. Other than the few properties along the bumpy road that was mainly a tract over rock, the way in was by boat. Most people had to park at the resort parking lot and launch at the docks and boat everything in. They paid for parking and launching or dock rental space, including the canoeists with permits to enter the park. Charlie had a good set up, he thought.

Dan thought the coming week-end should be busier on the lake and maybe at the resort too. The fall colours were at the peak he noticed when they drove in on Sunday, so the tourists and artists and hikers will be lured into the area. It's hard to say, though, with the recession-like economy still in full swing.

This was a new experience for him, coming like this in the fall. When they came at their usual time, the end of April into the first part of May, they were usually the only group at the resort. It was just getting ready to open after being closed all winter. He would greet Charlie looking at a fresh face, full of enthusiasm for the upcoming season. He could see now though, that working every day since the resort opened had taken its toll. He noticed there were lines of tiredness, exhaustion even, around Charlie's eyes and mouth.

It was Tuesday, the third day of Dan's trip. He had been

coming with a different group for 25 years, bringing the best and brightest of the fourth-year geology students with him. The area was ripe for geologists being in the La Cloche mountain area, known for its high quality white quartzite. A company was still mining it at a quarry at the edge of Highway 6 near the road into Miner's Village, to be broken down into the silica used to make glass.

Sometimes another professor would come if the numbers warranted it, but not this year. There were only five students this time. There was a mix up with funding and the usual spring trip was canceled. The money finally came in for a 10-day fall trip, but some students were already working after graduating and couldn't take the time off. Why would they if they had jobs in the field? The trip still included an extra credit though, and it was this and the field experience that when seen on a resume could help the students get a foot in the door.

Thank Christ none of this group had it in their heads that they would walk into a million-dollar-a-year job in the oil industry in Alberta as soon as they graduated. How he got through teaching the course in the 1990s with those students who thought like that, he had no idea. Most of them didn't have the love of seeing the wonders inside the rock. They just wanted the big offices and big windows in Calgary and the stake in the share of the oil companies who hired them. The boom of the oil industry in the seventies then again in the nineties meant graduates expected to be rich, finding high-paying jobs in the lucrative oil business right out of university. A lot did. This group this year though, would be lucky to find full-time work doing anything. The bust in the oil industry in

Alberta was happening.

He still had work though. The geology course was still part of Brock University's curriculum, for now. He could leave if he wanted with an early pension, but his divorce settlement would take a big chunk of that each month. Besides, at 62 he still thought of himself as young. What would he do if not teach? Isn't 60 the new 30s or something like that? he thought. He still had a trim and fit body from all the climbing around escarpments chipping away at rock and swimming twice a week at the community pool in St. Catherine's. It was this confidence and arrogance, he thought with a shudder, that led to his thinking that Ashley would welcome his arm around her when they were at the camp fire last night.

The other students drew dinner clean-up duty, so hadn't joined them outside yet. It was dark and there were a few trees between them and the cottage where the other students were washing dishes, so he was sure no one saw Ashley shove him away, or heard her hiss that he was "fucked, so fucked." She said she would report harassment to the university once they were back and he could kiss what remained of his pension good-bye. His recent divorce was no secret among the students or staff. Ashley made it clear it was only her fear of losing the course credit that would stop her from saying anything to anyone during the rest of the time on the field trip. She got up and stormed into the cottage to join the others.

The students all come out to the campfire shortly after that. Ashley sat close to Lori on the bench by the fire. Dan stayed for a beer then left them to it saying goodnight, taking refuge in his cottage. He closed all the curtains, poured more than his usual shot of whisky, glad that the liquor store in Espanola carried Jameson Irish Whiskey and that they stopped in on the way to the resort. He sat in the dark thinking how he could change Ashley's mind to report him, or to change her version to one of innocence on his part.

Now though, it was time for him to get dressed for the day. They were going to take the van along Highway 6 and stop for rock samples at different spots, the same spots he took the students each year. This time though, there was no need for bug repellent, and the terrain would be dry and not snow-soaked and muddy. He put on his canvass cargo pants with the zippers at the knees and a long-sleeved button-up shirt with sleeves he could roll up past his elbows and button once the day got warmer. The day looked promising with no forecast of rain. He might be able to unzip his pants to shorts. He found he got hot quickly hiking and working on sun-warmed rocks. He took down his Tilley hat from the peg on the wall by the door and packed it with his backpack already organized with what he needed for the day.

He made his bed and rinsed out his coffee cup. He looked around the little one-room cottage thinking this trip could be his last if Ashley did report him. He loved the cottage. He always stayed in this one. It had a blue swivel chair, a queen-sized bed and an antique wood dresser painted blue with red hearts, all in the same room as the kitchen. Everything was in good repair and always clean. Though small, the kitchen was fully equipped and had an old wood table for two, set into one corner of the room. It was set with a red and white gingham cloth and an old creamer filled with fresh flowers or flowering weeds found on the property and picked by Charlie. Windows all around the cottage and a back door including its own screen door, afforded the views of the mixed-growth forest that surrounded the resort. He put on his leather hiking boots, careful to tuck the bottom of his pants into his socks for protection against the first-of-the-day chill and dampness on the ground.

He would go sit in the screened front porch for a bit then go knocking at the other two cottages along the lake to wake up the students. It was almost time for everyone to get cooking and eating breakfast.

They always met in cottage #1 where the three male students were staying, each with their own bedroom. It was the largest cottage on the resort with a wood harvest table large enough to fit them all with room to spare this year. Ashley was sharing cottage #2 with Lori. It had three bedrooms too, but not the space in the living area or at the table. Like his cottage, it had electric baseboard heating but no wood stove like in cottage #1.

He could now see the smoke coming out of the chimney, so one of the boys must be up already. It was probably Peter, he seemed to be more on the ball in the mornings than Haiden and Greg.

He liked that his cottage was set back behind and between cottages #1 and #2. His cottage was built last, well after numbers one through five were built spaced well apart along the lake, each with private docks. The hill was too steep at the far end of the shoreline for any more buildings so cottage #6 was built at the next best spot. There was still a full view of the lake in front though, and the cottage was surrounded by white pines and a few cedar trees. He could see what the students were up to for the most part. He could see them walking between the cottages and see the lights come on or go off inside.

He hoped he didn't have to knock to wake up the girls. He didn't know how he was going to face Ashley this morning and wondered if she kept her promise or if she confided in Lori.

CHAPTER 4

Charlie

It was 7:45 am and time to get a move on. Charlie turned off the computer, reluctantly got up from the warm leather chair at the desk that faced out to the lake, walked over to the wood stove, slipped out of the moccasins and slipped into the tall, green Hunter boots that had been warming beside the fire. It was supposed to get warm today with no indication of rain, but the pine needles and long grass and weeds by the lake shore would be soaking wet still. Charlie walked to the other side of the room down a short hallway, and put on the wind jacket hanging beside the door that was marked 'private' on the exterior, for the house part of the resort only. The sign didn't seem to deter guests from trying to come in that way, but Charlie thought an effort should be made to try to stop them. After a quick grab to put on the thick gloves with the leather hand and finger grips that were on the chair by the door, Charlie went outside.

The nuthatches were busy traveling down the trees, upside down to the other birds flitting about and on the branches of the tall pines that grew thick in front of the house and office. Their chatter amused Charlie, and the smell of the pine needles was exhilarating. This is why Charlie bought the resort here three seasons ago. Most of the landscape appeared unspoiled, even though logging and mining was going on years ago. The rail line along the opposite shore built by INCO to pick up mine workers from a small enclave of company houses was still there, but not used by trains anymore. Originally there was no road in from Highway 6 to the houses. There was now. Most of the 12 houses not occupied by somebody whose family had 'always lived there', were rented out by owners to weekenders. Guests coming to stay with Charlie at Kirk Lake Camp used the road, as did cottagers heading for the few properties that dotted the shore, just past Creepyville. Charlie smiled at the name given the village by one of the guests a few years ago. This was because of the line of attached dilapidated garages that lined both sides of the road coming into the area. Most of the garages were not used and had doors hanging off the hinges or sagging with rot. The roofs were covered in lichen and pine needles and old maple branches that fell from the trees that almost enveloped the buildings. Since then, Charlie didn't think of the area by its real name, Miners' Village, though it wasn't populated enough to be called a real village. There were no services for the residents other than the neighbouring volunteer fire department or O.P.P. police that had to come in from the highway if patrolling nearby, or from the station just outside of Espanola on Highway 17. That was about a 20 minute drive away, if traffic wasn't stopped by a beaver or a turtle crossing the road. That was the extent of the traffic jam up here.

This final section of the drive to the resort through the village was not the prettiest first impression for Charlie's guests, after the first part of the drive, along the two km. section of roller-coaster hills and turns cut into the side of the towering hill of quartzite rock in hues of white, pinks, burgundies and grays. On one side of the road was the steep rock face. The other side bordered a steep drop-off, with only one small section of guard rail and a bit of shoulder with room for one car to pull over. The view of the lake and surrounding hills and forest was magnificent, so it was usual to see a car parked there.

Charlie walked the 20 or so strides from the house to the dock, being careful to step over the exposed tree roots, and stepped onto the pontoon boat. It would be good to warm the motor a bit this morning, so Charlie started the motor first, then got busy at the white stacking chairs. They should have been resting upside down against the railings along the sides of the boat. They had been moved and not put back, so Charlie had to wipe them down again. A wet bum would teach them a lesson, she thought, but knew she could never do that to them.

No sooner had Charlie dried the chairs and set them four to a side along the 32' pontoon boat, which was really a deck on pontoons, when the drake and his ducklings came walking along the shore to the boat.

"Good morning Charlie," said Professor Bowen as he led his charge up the dock and onto the boat. "It's going to be a great day!"

"Good morning. Hi everyone!" answered Charlie, first

smiling at Dan then looking at the five sullen-looking students.

A mix of "morn'n" "hi" "hey" and mostly mumbling meant the students were bagged from a late night of drinking instead of studying, or maybe just shy. Probably drinking, thought Charlie, remembering the loud voices by the fire the night before. Well, well, love is in the air. Charlie saw that Haiden moved his chair closer to where Ashley was sitting. It wasn't a real surprise since he did the same thing the past two days on the boat trip to and from the landing. It wasn't a big surprise, either, to see the look that quickly passed between Ashley and Lori, who sat across from her. It seemed Ashley was not as keen on Haiden as he was on her.

Peter and Greg chose to stand, facing the front, setting their legs apart to keep their balance for the five minute boat ride across to the resort parking lot. Neither would give the other the pleasure of seeing them hold onto the railing. Charlie's eyes rolled at the absurdity of this male competition.

The professor sat in his usual spot, as close to the front of the boat deck as he knew was allowed. There was no railing across the front and Charlie didn't like anyone up too close to the end. Charlie had once seen a little pontoon boat go under the water when too many large people were sitting on the deck at the front, feet hanging over the edge. A large wave from the wake of a passing boat caught the top of the deck and tipped the boat under, people included.

The professor's chair faced the front. When he first met Charlie he explained by saying he liked to "feel the full wind in his sails". Charlie sensed it would take more than that to perk him up today. He had a bit of a mood about him this morning and noted the tone of his voice didn't match his jubilant words. He looked a bit pale and tired, and older. Well, Charlie was older too since they first met three years ago.

Maybe he's tiring of this trip Charlie thought, but hoped not, since the university money came in handy when there wasn't as much money in the bank at the start of the season. By September, the money wasn't as big an issue since the resort still did well through the summer. It didn't really matter when the money came in, as long as it came in, so Charlie agreed to the September trip. It meant, though, the fall solitude would be broken with the students on the property. There would be no sleeping in either, after the busy summer. Charlie would have to be ready to boat the group over to their van every morning at 8:00 am and be there to pick them up at 5:00 pm Charlie was stuck working around their schedule for the remainder of their stay.

CHAPTER 5

Bob

He watched Charlie on the boat. He saw the students come out of the cottages, the girls out of cottage #2 and the boys out of cottage #1. He wondered again why Charlie didn't come up with something more original on the signs on the cottages thinking that people would like something other than a number. Either way, he didn't like that they were there. A few quiet guests would likely come on the last few week-ends of the season. He noticed the couple in cottage #5 who came on Sunday were still there, probably for the peak of the fall colours, but Charlie was usually alone through the week this time of year. The groups of fishing guys would come a bit later, toward the end of September and into October for Thanksgiving, when the bass would be bigger and tastier as the lake turned with the cold fall nights. Then no one would come until May next year. That's what he liked.

He watched the girls come down the steps from the screened porch. They looked like city girls wearing tight tops, little jackets and tight jeans. They looked like they were heading to a bar and not going traipsing around the rocks They were wearing hiking boots at least, he noticed, and one was wearing a cap. He watched the one with the long dark hair look over her shoulder at the boys walking along from cottage #1 up behind them. Two of the boys called out something making both girls turn and laugh. He saw the laughter die on the dark-hair girl's face as she looked at the other boy. He didn't seem to notice or care though. He ran ahead and walked close beside her. He saw that she moved her arm away from him to hold onto the knapsack she had slung over her other shoulder. He watched the boy's hand brush the girl's hip as they came to a narrow part of the path along the shore between the two old cedar trees. He could almost feel the soft hip.

He moved the binoculars back to where Charlie was putting the last chair into place on the boat. Charlie looked over suddenly. He put the binoculars down.

CHAPTER 6

Dan

Dan stopped to look at the view from the landing across the 400 metre stretch of water to the resort he had come to love. The lake returned to its flat state after Charlie dropped them off headed back. The last of the wake from the boat was hitting the shore with a sucking sound, the splash back taking some of the earth with it. He liked to walk in the water along the shore and look under the little caves created, but he was also pleased to see that Charlie had let the grass and weeds grow long along the shores as much as possible. In the last years he could see the progress of the shoreline going back to a natural state. It meant being startled by more water snakes coming out of the tall grasses to the sunny spots where they would sit coiled up for hours, sometimes with a noticeable bulge, digesting a mouse, but Dan preferred this to the grass being mowed right to the edge of the shoreline like many lakefront property owners did.

He noticed that Charlie made sure to slow the boat well in advance of docking it to help prevent further erosion. He remembered the previous owner operating the boat at full throttle and jamming the motor into reverse just shy of the dock, probably to give the students a bit of a jarring after a late-night knock at the office door for a deck of cards or something. Charlie was more careful mooring the boat, he thought with a smile, knowing there was a sign attached to the front of the dock, "No Mooring." Though meant to detract the boaters that would otherwise take up the longest dock reserved for the pontoon boat alone, the sign only piqued the question, "What does mooring mean?" from almost every student he has brought to the resort since Charlie hammered in the sign.

Will this be my last trip? Dan wondered, until Haiden called to him from the side door of the van where he was seated beside Ashley.

"Are you coming? We're not going to get anywhere without a driver."

Dan thought he knew why Haiden was in such a hurry. He was probably hoping to get some alone time with Ashley like he did yesterday when they had their first field trip. Dan caught Haiden trying to get Ashley out of sight of the others, motioning to her to "Come and check this out Ash" more times than he cared to hear. He knew Ashley did not like Haiden. The rest of the group laughed about his dogged attempts to seduce her when they met in the university pub to discuss the trip up north. Haiden laughed too. He didn't seem daunted by her rebuffs.

Dan thought about that last pub night when he and Ashley were alone at the table for a few minutes while the others got their beer order in. He was sure that Ashley preferred him. No, not just preferred, but wanted him. She drank more than usual that night, he remembered. Perhaps she didn't remember flirting with him and brushing her arm up against his and making those almost lewd comments about younger women and older men having sex. Shit, thought Dan. He will have to get Ashley alone and talk her out of reporting him when they get back to the university. That was the only way out of this mess now.

CHAPTER 7

Charlie

Charlie went upstairs to the kitchen and put some oatmeal on to cook before going into the bedroom and getting changed out of the long underwear and wind pants into canvas work pants and a tee-shirt. While at the dresser Charlie saw a flash of something reflected in the mirror above. It seemed to come from the front bedroom window, almost like the flash of light that caught Charlie's eye from across the lake just before the students boarded the boat. Charlie looked out the window but only saw waves of sunlight reflecting on the water.

After breakfast and clean-up, Charlie went back down the stairs into the office. The retired couple that were staying in cottage #5 all week, Jack and Edna Porter, were coming in the office door just as Charlie opened the interior door that separated the office from the private portion of the main floor and entered the room.

"Hi Charlie," said Edna. "We thought we would take the fishing boat down the lake and have a picnic on one of the islands. Can we have a map of the lake to take with us? So you don't worry, we will be gone most of the day. If we need to get across to the car we'll take the fishing boat over ourselves so we won't bother you."

"Do you have any worms in? I saw the bait fridge on the front porch was empty," asked Jack quickly with a defiant look at Edna, before Charlie had a chance to answer Edna.

"Sure Edna, here's the map," said Charlie, pulling one from the counter drawer.

Looking at Jack, Charlie said, "It's that time of year. There's no need for me to keep that fridge plugged in for the few guests here until I close up for the season. I have some upstairs in my fridge in the kitchen. I will get you some. One, or two tubs?"

"Two," said Jack, his face a picture of hope at his fishing chances.

"One," said Edna at the same time, sensing her picnic time shortening and the fishing time lengthening.

"One it is," said Charlie, going upstairs, leaving Edna pleased that Charlie took her side and Jack chuffed.

Charlie came back down with a container of worms and a brown paper bag.

"I'll add it to your tab," Charlie said, and gave the worms and bag to Jack. "It's that fishing book you let me borrow last year. I set it aside for you."

Edna, not the slightest bit interested in anything to do with fishing, walked out of the office ahead of Jack, ready to get going to spend time on the water with her camera and sketch pad. Jack peaked inside the bag, saw the second container of worms, gave Charlie a wink, and followed Edna.

The landing phone rang, startling Charlie.

"Hello?"

"Hello. I am waiting for a pick-up so I come over to check on the water system," said a man with a strong Scottish accent.

"Okay. I'll be right there," said Charlie and hung up. There was a phone at the parking lot that rang into one of the office phones to let Charlie know when the boat was needed. It used to ring on a loud speaker system that could be heard all along the 1500' of shoreline and back and beyond. If Charlie was at the other end of the property from the office, that meant the ringing was non-stop until Charlie walked back to the office to pick up the receiver. That annoyed Charlie and the guests, so after the first season, Charlie had the phone line switched to ring only inside the office. The portable phone could then be carried all around the property and be answered from anywhere.

At the landing, a man emerged from an older, black, pick-up truck parked near the dock. He wore a kilt of green, blue, and yellow tartan with a cream coloured wool sweater under an expensive-looking black wind-jacket. Gray wool socks with a red and white stripe showed above his worn and scuffed Kodiak work boots. He carried a tool box. He walked to the dock, jumped aboard the front of the boat, pulled a black, wool watchman's cap from his jacket pocket and put it on his head that was sparse of gray hair but neatly cut short. He planted his feet apart, and stood near the railing. His face lit up with a smile that started from his light blue eyes and ended in a wide grin, accenting the deep lines around his eyes and mouth.

"Hello Charlene," he said.

CHAPTER 8

Bob

He rinsed out his coffee mug and took his toast to the table by the window that he used as a desk. He moved the binoculars aside, opened his lap top, found the file, opened it, and looked at the pictures slowly, one at a time.

He heard the boat motor and saw Charlie docking the pontoon boat. He watched the man follow her up to the house. He smiled, knowing what would come next.

CHAPTER 9

Dan

"I'm sorry Ashley. I misread what I thought was interest in me. You were all over me at the pub before the trip!" Dan said when he finally had a chance with Ashley alone out of earshot from the other students.

"What! You've got to be kidding me!" said Ashley, her whisper not masking her tone of disgust. "I have no interest in you whatsoever!"

"Look, it was inappropriate and I'm really sorry. It was just a hug, not that I'm saying that it was okay to do that," Dan added quickly when he saw that Ashley was about to retort.

"Please Ashley, I'm begging you! Don't report what happened. Nothing like that will happen again."

"I guess not! Once this course is over I won't have to be near you again. I've already graduated, but you know how important this course is for my resume! That's the only reason I haven't said anything to anyone yet," Ashley said. "And I mean yet. You can't get away with touching students!"

"Please Ashley," he said.

"No way Professor Bowen! You need to be held accountable." Ashley picked up her tools and knapsack and walked quickly away, not looking back when Dan said, "You bitch! You're going to regret your decision."

"What?" she asked over her shoulder.

The professor said nothing more, and Ashley walked away over the rocky trail to join the others. He saw her jump back as she almost bumped into Haiden who jumped down in front of her from a rock overhang.

CHAPTER 10

Charlene

"Is that appropriate attire to check on my water pump?" Charlene asked.

"It's not the pipes I'll be looking at," said Joe.

"You know the saying," Charlene said as she took Joe's hand and led him up the stairs to the house. "Let's see what's under that kilt sir."

"Are you saying you got me here to check on my Scottishness?" asked Joe.

"I didn't ask you here at all," answered Charlene

"No, but now that I'm here..." Joe picked up Charlene and carried her down the hall of the house and took her to the bedroom.

CHAPTER 11

Bob

He left his desk and walked down to his dock. He carried his life jacket, paddle and fishing rod that he stored in the shed beside the cottage. He checked that he also brought the box of fishing line he bought at Walmart when he went to Sudbury last week. The Spiderwire Ultracast Ultimate 10 pound line may come in handy soon. It better, for $14.00 a box. He usually bought 20 pound line for only $3.00 for almost as many yards when he used to go fishing with the guys from work out on Ranger Lake, but the line on his rod was old and probably wouldn't work for what he had in mind.

He remembered to get the worms from his fridge on his way out. There were still a few worms left in the container he bought at that little bait shop he found one day while driving around Espanola. He knew it would be much easier to buy his worms from Charlie but he was not ready to be that close to her yet.

He flipped the bright yellow kayak over and bent down and looked inside it. Not much bothered him, but a water snake or dock spider coming up at him from inside the kayak would. It would not be a good start to what would be a pleasant paddle along the shoreline with his fishing line in the lake behind him with hopes of a nice bass lunch.

He put his life jacket under the tension cords on top of the kayak. It was going to be too warm to wear it. He pulled the kayak to the dock and put it in the water and tied it to one of the cleats, noticing the end of the rope was getting frayed. He would have to remember to put a match to it to melt it. He should also remember to get marine rope next time he was in Canadian Tire, he thought. The cheap blue rope from the Dollar Store wasn't holding up. He was new to all this boating stuff. He was a city dweller, living in Sault Ste. Marie, aka the Soo, all his life, until he bought his cottage. He got it for a good deal from an old guy who had it for about 50 years before it got to be too much for him to keep up. It came with an old 14' fishing boat and a pretty good, but old, 9.9hp Johnson motor. He wrote his boating exam and passed and now just had to learn how to dock the boat better. He found it tricky in the wind, and it was almost always windy in front of his place.

He didn't stay at the cottage all year. The winters would be too isolated. He would head to a rental trailer in a park in Panama City Beach with a bunch of other oldies for a few months until mid-April when he came back to the lake. He was one of the youngest at the park at 60-years-old. He retired from Essar Steel almost two years ago when he was offered a good package and hasn't regretted it. The money from the sale of his house in the Soo paid for the cottage with lots left over, and his work pension would give him enough to live comfortably, if he was careful, for the rest of his life. He handled his divorce the right way five years ago, and she would get no more money from him. Five more years and his Canada Pension and Old Age Security would kick in and he could upgrade to a better trailer. Hell, he thought, he may even put his name in for a trailer at a ritzy park right on the ocean.

He thought he would stay at the lake few more months this year, depending on how his plan unraveled.

He got into the kayak and untied the rope, leaving bits of blue on his hands and on the dock. He pushed off. He liked the way the kayak moved in the water, stable and strong even in the high winds that usually picked up on the narrow lake around mid-day.

He liked that it was the exact kayak as Charlie's. He loved to watch her pull her yellow kayak off the storage rack, drag it along the path, then carry it along the dock and set it into the water.

He could see some gray streaks in her fair hair when the wind tossed it about her face and neckline, so he knew she was not young. The powerful binoculars also picked up the creases around her eyes and mouth and the deep wrinkle along the one side of her jaw line. She had brown age and sun spots and lots of freckles. He noticed she usually wore a long-sleeved button down shirt like you see in the fishing shows from Florida. Too much sun in the past he thought. She wore sunglasses most of the time when on the water so he couldn't see her eyes. He admired her athleticism and grace though as she got in and out of the kayak at the side of the dock. She was trim and he thought she must be fit from all the work she did around the resort, even with hired help from Sam McGregor, the young guy from the reserve half-way down the highway to Little Current. He was known locally as a good handyman, that is when he showed up, and when he wanted to be. He often saw him up high on a ladder painting the resort cottages. Lots of times he saw him fishing off the dock with a smoke hanging off the corner of his mouth when Charlie wasn't around.

He steadied his kayak. It was difficult for him to get in. His heavy 6', 230 pound frame was built more for stepping on and off a pontoon boat then getting in a small hole in a kayak that rocked on the water when he got in and out of it. He was still getting used to that. He liked that he might be on the water the same time as Charlie though. He took his binoculars with him always just in case she decided on a paddle. That didn't happen very much in the summer months, but now she had a bit more time with fewer guests and the students gone for the day and he didn't want to miss the chance.

CHAPTER 12

Dan

The students seem to have remembered what they learned
yesterday for the most part. It shouldn't be so hard for them
to grasp, Dan thought. They'd been out on a few field trips in
southern Ontario. It was part of the course though, the review
of field techniques, including orientation, use of a compass, and
pacing and measurement of Cross beds. The layers within the
rocks in the La Cloche hills and along the high rock faces at
the side of Highway 6 where the rock was blasted to make way
for the highway, were clearly visible. There was no need to go
over what they were, the layers known as cross strata. What
the students had to figure out though, and clearly present in
their reports, was what the layers reveal to geologists about
ancient times in the area, including the paleocurrents, or wind
direction of ancient flow within the rock.

Today they were examining the basal conformity of the
Huronia succession with the Archean basement. That was
keeping them busy the professor thought, as he stretched his
strong, athletic legs out in front of him as he sat on the warm

rock. He removed the bottom of his pants earlier and was more comfortable with just shorts. He couldn't believe the difference in working outside now rather than in the spring. The pine needles gave off a heady fragrance as the heat of the day hit the wooded areas that meandered through the hill and over the rocks.

He needed time alone to think. He uncapped his thermos to have some green tea. What he really wanted was a belt of whisky, wishing he tucked the Jameson bottle into his knapsack. The talk with Ashley didn't go the way he hoped it would. Her refusal to listen and her determination to go through with a harassment complaint, made him feel physically sick. That, and the sudden appearance of Haiden. He must have overheard some, if not all, of the exchange between him and Ashley. Now he may have to deal with Haiden too.

Dan remembered that tonight was pub night. He would escort the students into the little restaurant just off the highway after they had a chance to get back to the resort and clean up. He forgot to ask Charlie if it was okay if she took them over to the landing again about 7:00 p.m. and then picked them up late after the pub. She had done it in the past so he didn't think it would be a problem, but he was normally more courteous and let her know ahead of time. The wings at the Black Cat pub were so good he didn't want to bow out. It might be his last wing dinner if he lost his job. He wouldn't lose his job though, he thought. He would get fined or something, wouldn't he? Maybe the university would no longer fund the trip. He could take that, even though he'd miss coming up here. Maybe Charlie would like some help running the place and he could stay up here for the summer. Probably not. Sam seemed pretty settled in.

Dan thought he would ask Charlie if he could take a fishing boat out tomorrow just in case it was his last chance to be out on the beautiful lake, so beautiful that much of it had been painted by a couple of artists in the famous Group of Seven. Thursday and Friday would be spent in Sudbury at an INCO site, then into Elliot Lake touring the decommissioned mine areas and tailing ponds. Tomorrow though, maybe he could drive Lori's car and lead the students to the field site and leave them on their own. Peter could drive the van and follow him, Lori lived in Sudbury when not in university, and was visiting her parents just before the trip, so she drove her own car to meet the rest of the group at the resort on Sunday. They're adults for Christ's sake. He'd talk to Charlie when they got back.

He could even see if Charlie had a spare fishing pole. And, he brightened up, if Ashley drank as much beer tonight as she did at the university pub before the trip, maybe he could talk some sense into her and it would all work out.

Dan heard the geese before he saw them. He lost count at 35 in the V formation. That was a sure sign of fall. It was also a sign it was near the end of the day and time to drive back. He brushed off the maple keys that had fallen onto his shirt and knapsack, leaving them for the evening grosbeaks and ruffed grouse to eat, and got up to corral the students.

CHAPTER 13

Charlene

As Charlene heated up some homemade pumpkin and apple soup, she knew her window of spending more time with Joe was almost up. Edna and Jack were away for the day, and the students wouldn't be back until 5:00 p.m., but a group was due to arrive soon to rent canoes for a three-day trip into the provincial park.

"I know you're looking at the clock Charlene," Joe said as he smiled and wrapped his arms around her in the kitchen after their showers. "I better go downstairs and look at the water system for you like I said I would. I think the ultra-violet light will need a cleaning."

Charlene stayed upstairs and set a nice table for their lunch in front of the large window that overlooked the trees and lake. The house was on the second floor of the resort building built into the slope of a steep hill. The office was in half of the first floor for guests. The other half was private, for storage of linens and supplies. Being on a water-access property, there was no time to drive into Espanola every time supplies were needed, so Charlene kept a good stock of what she knew by now were the essentials. There were two washers and two dryers to handle the heavy loads of laundering of the sheets and blankets supplied for the guests.

The water-treatment area was at the back of the first floor, where Charlene could hear Joe whistling some ditty or other. The previous owners said the well water was good and always tested clean, but the post Walkerton water disaster meant new rules for public drinking water so Charlene had state-of-the-art equipment installed, taking no risks that anyone, including herself, would get sick from drinking or cooking with bad water.

The house was up some stairs from the storage area and had a level back door walk-out to the cleared area and woods behind the house. During the season Charlene mainly used this door to get to her own garbage bin and to sneak outside so guests wouldn't see her before the office was open. There was a deck at the front of the house going the full 60' along the second-floor. She had a local contractor, who was looking for cash-in-hand in the slow season, build the covered deck so she could see the lake and be among the maple branches and pine boughs. They gave a lot of privacy and protection from the sun at the height of summer. Of course, for most of the time the resort was open, being outside meant mostly being in the one half of the deck that was screened-in, accessed from the kitchen through a patio sliding door.

This was not that time of year though. The bugs were gone, at least until the next late batch of black flies, usually in October. They were mostly just showy then, and didn't bite as much. The mosquitoes haven't been around since about the third week in August. From spring to summer, if a bug was out it would find her. She would be a bloody mess when the black flies got around her hair and neck while she was up a ladder or doing something where she couldn't swat at them. The mosquitoes weren't a bother during the day though because the wind coming across the lake could breeze through the trees along the front of the property. The low boughs had been cut by the previous owners and though she didn't like the idea at first, she quickly came to understand and appreciate the reasoning behind it. Charlene didn't spend much time outside at dusk when the mosquitoes were at their biting worst. She tried only going out then when she had to. If a guest needed something like a boat ride over to the landing or a replacement propane tank she provided for the barbeques, she sprayed herself liberally with Muskol, the product that seemed to work better than the others. She moved quickly and the return guests understood her rush, knowing how vulnerable she was to any biting insects. This, Charlene thought, was another thing she got from her Dad. He too could get quite puffy and have bad reactions to bug bites.

While waiting for Joe to finish his work, Charlene made a batch of biscuits from scratch. She threw in some raisins and fresh cranberries, liking the flavour pairing with the soup. It made her think of Thanksgiving flavours. She thought of how much more time the two of them could spend together when Joe would finally retire from his winter job and the resort would be closed after the Thanksgiving week-end.

Charlene liked having a man around the house. She smiled

at the memory of the two of them taking a blanket to the cleared area in the woods behind the house a few years ago. It was on a fall day that was not unlike this one. They stretched out in the sun after taking off their clothes and making love. And that's what it really was then, the day she thinks they both realized they could be in love with each other. When the late sun started to chill them, Charlene started to get dressed but Joe stopped her and threw her clothes onto the blanket.

"My boots good sir," said Charlene.

"Ah yes, the tender toes," said Joe as he passed her the tall rubber boots she often wore. He put on his own hiking boots, gathered up the blanket over his shoulder, and they walked naked, hand-in-hand, toward the house.

"If your guests could see you now Ms. Parker, they would be aghast," he said.

"If your customers could see you now Mr. McFadden, they'd be asking for the same service," Charlene said.

CHAPTER 14

Bob

When he returned from a short paddle, disappointed he didn't catch any fish, he saw Charlie take Joe back across the lake. He didn't need his binoculars to recognize him. Who else wore a kilt around here? He thought it odd at first then came to appreciate the uniqueness of it and found he was disappointed when Joe didn't wear it. He also liked the Saturday evening ritual in the summer months when Joe would stand at the end of the long dock at the resort parking lot and play the bagpipes. He heard the pipes the first Saturday when he took possession of the cottage at the beginning of July last year. He just got settled in with a drink on the deck after moving his personal items into the furnished cottage when he heard the unmistakable sound of bagpipes being warmed up. He looked over at the resort but couldn't see where the sound was coming from. He looked down the lake and saw a man in full Scottish attire standing at the end of the long dock at the resort parking lot. By then the piping had begun and it carried on every Saturday night during the summer months just before dusk, for about 15 minutes. The guests at the resort seemed to enjoy it, getting in their boats and canoes and coming across the lake to get a closer look, or standing on the docks at or along the shore at the resort. They usually clapped when Joe stopped, though he was never sure whether it was out of appreciation for the music or because Joe was finished playing and got in his truck and drove off.

When he took his generator in for repairs a few weeks after that to the little shop not far down the highway, he realized the repair guy was the piper. It would be too much of a coincidence for him to see two tall, lean men in their late fifties with sparse gray hair, in the same area, wearing the same tartan kilt. He caught him just leaving the shop that was adjacent to a small square-timber house at the end of a long spit of land surrounded by Georgian Bay waters. He was friendly and introduced himself as Joe, and opened the shop back up so the generator could be wheeled in. He had the trouble sorted out within a few minutes and it was fixed on the spot, surprising him with the strength and speed of his hands and fingers. After that he saw Joe coming and going from the resort and thought he was doing repairs for Charlie. He saw them together at a restaurant in Little Current this spring though, and noticed a closeness between them. Seeing the way they looked at each other he put two and two together and realized they were a couple.

He jumped back from the desk nearly knocking his chair over when he heard footsteps outside. He saw Joe coming around the corner of the cottage along the deck to the front patio doors. He also saw that Joe was looking right at him through the glass of the door when he slammed down the top of his laptop before walking the few steps to the door.

"Hello Bob," said Joe.

"Hey Joe," he answered.

"Sorry I startled you," Joe said. "I thought I'd bring your whipper snipper back. It works just fine now. There was a bit of old line stuck where he shouldn't have been stuck."

"You didn't need to bring it here. I could have come to get it," said Bob

"I had some work to do at Charlene's so thought I would save you the bother," said Joe.

"Charlene?" asked Bob

"Yes," said Joe.

"Who's Charlene?" asked Bob.

"Charlene Parker, the owner of Kirk Lake Camp, you know, your neighbour across the lake," said Joe. "Don't tell me you've not yet met her!"

"No. She always seems so busy. I thought her name was Charlie. The young guy in the yard at the Home Hardware in Espanola called her Charlie. I was telling him where to deliver a load of lumber I needed to fix my dock last fall and he said he knew where my cottage was since he delivered to Charlie at the resort all the time. He said she was really nice and let him launch his boat for free anytime," Bob said.

"I remember correcting him by saying he must have meant he, but he said Charlie was a she."

"Ah," said Joe starting to understand Bob's confusion. "It's a nickname given to her a long time ago by a co-worker. He was into jazz and Charlie Parker Jr. When she changed her name back after her divorce, her co-worker couldn't resist the nickname. I never call her Charlie, knowing she prefers Charlene, so I forget that others do."

"Was it a co-worker from Hamilton Police? I heard she used to be a detective," Bob asked.

"If you want to know more about her, I suggest you introduce yourself to her. She would be happy to meet her closest neighbor," said Joe, just before he noticed the large and expensive-looking binoculars on the desk. He looked over his shoulder and saw that the resort was directly across the lake. Feeling uneasy, he bade Bob a good day. Bob saw him look toward the desk again. He wasn't worried though. He remembered he had closed his laptop.

CHAPTER 15

Dan

Dan waited in the office for Charlie to be finished with the group gathered around the counter. They all had thick Scottish accents and he heard a snippet of their conversation when he walked into the office after explaining, yet again, to the students what their assignment was, and to get cracking on it before they went to the pub.

He found himself smiling as he heard one of the men say they were from Scotland, here to explore a bit of northern Ontario. Dan had been to some parts of Scotland and he found the terrain around the resort reminded him of some of the landscape of the northern isles with the steep rock faces along the water and hills everywhere.

The three men and three women looked like couples, as they talked about who would go in what canoe with whom and for how long. The women clearly in charge. Hopefully one of them drew up a schedule so they could switch canoe partners and get away from their spouses for a bit. They way they were rolling their eyes as the men talked about their paddling skills and how they could probably portage the canoes without the help of the women, made Dan almost laugh out loud. Wait until they see the steep incline and the length of the first portage into the park and up to the next lake! They are getting a late start too. No paddler in their right mind starts a trek in September at 5:00 pm They'd probably have to camp along the shore at the bottom of the portage, if they even got that far before dark.

He watched Charlie size them all up for paddles and life jackets. The women gathered the safety kits, probably to tie up somewhere safe in the canoes, rather than leave it to the men to just throw them in. Dan had watched his own students when they took some canoes out for a break from studies and knew the women were almost always more organized then the men. The guys were apt to throw everything in the canoe and push off from the dock, often leaving safety kits or life jackets on the dock, not concerned about safety or the law. The girls would be kneeling or sitting on the padded life jackets comfortably, smirking at the guys' discomfort after a few hours on the lake. That reminded him, he better tell Greg not to take Charlie's kayak out again without asking permission. He saw him out on the lake Monday evening with it and saw the way Charlie watched him from shore and could tell she wasn't happy about it. That was for her own use and not for guests. He was surprised at the sense of entitlement Greg had, obviously going into the office when Charlie was not around and taking the kayak paddle from the rack of canoe paddles behind the counter. This was after he told the students not to take any boat or canoe without her permission. Dan meant to say something to Greg that night after dinner, but the situation with Ashley at the fire pit made him forget all about it.

The group looked like they were ready to leave the office.

"Do you need me up here Dan?" asked Charlene. "Can it wait until I get everyone settled into the canoes?"

"Sure. In fact I will walk down with you if I may. It is too nice an evening to be inside," said Dan.

Dan stood back and watched while Charlie had everyone inspect the three Nova Craft canoes already lined up along the shore in front of cottage #1, close to the large structure used for storing the canoes and Charlie's kayak. There would be no damages to the canoes. Dan knew she maintained all the boats, fixing anything as soon as it was needed. He had seen her tightening bolts and fixing sinew seats in the canoes many times.

Once the canoeists were out on the water and paddling away from the dock, Dan asked Charlie about her taking his group to the landing for pub night and picking them up at 11:00 pm

"Sure," she said, though by the look that passed in her eyes quickly, Dan thought what she would really have liked to say was, "Shit." He knew he better not ask for free use of a fishing boat now.

"I'd like to rent a fishing boat for the day tomorrow. I'm thinking of sending the students out alone tomorrow. I'll see if I can drive Lori's car and have Peter drive the van and follow me to the field site. I'll come back about 10:00 am and be ready to use the boat for the rest of the day."

"You'll have to take the fishing boat to the landing in the morning yourself then Dan. I have an appointment in

Espanola around 10:30 am and will be gone most of the day, so I won't be here to pick you up in the pontoon boat. You can dock the boat and leave it at the landing when I boat the students over. If we do the paperwork up now and if I top you up with gas, you'll be set in the morning," said Charlene.

"Would you happen to have an old fishing rod I could use?" Dan asked with what he thought was his most charming smile.

"I have a rod, but no line on it. I have a box of 10 pound line in the office. You are welcome to thread it on the rod and use it and just bring it back when you are finished with it. Do you want to take a container of worms too?" asked Charlene.

"Yes, thanks. I would have forgotten to take some worms," said Dan as they walked back into the office, and he waited while Charlie went upstairs to get the worms and return.

She rummaged around in the drawers behind the office counter and gave Dan the box of fishing line.

"Hmm. Spiderwire. I've never heard of this brand," said Dan.

"I got an order in this spring and only have two more boxes left on the shelf. They are expensive but the guests were asking for it and it really sold well," Charlene said as she walked over to the small assortment of fishing tackle available for sale along the back wall of the office.

"That's odd. I don't see them anywhere."

"It looks like someone has written down on your tab sheet a box of Spiderwire line," said Dan as he wrote his name and a container of worms on the sheet of paper on the counter in front of him. He liked that Charlie asked guests to take what they wanted from the small store in the office and write their name, cottage number and the item on a tab sheet and settle the bill later. He guessed it was more convenient for her instead of having to be stuck in the office or having to stop what she was doing all the time to walk back to the office for every small transaction. The students especially were amazed by the trust she showed them and seemed reluctant to follow her request to just take and sign and pay later. They didn't grow up with small stores giving credit like he and Charlie did so they were not used to it.

"It looks like Greg signed for a box. He likes to get out on the dock and fish when we get back from the field trips," said Dan, thinking again that he better talk to Greg about keeping himself and his fishing rod out of Charlie's kayak. "I can't make out the signature for the other box though."

"Let's see that sheet."

Dan noticed the look of surprise pass over Charlie's face when she looked at the signature.

"Do you know who it is?" he asked.

"Yes I do. It's a friend of mine. He was here earlier today to check on the water system."

"Okay. We will see you at the dock at 7:00 o'clock. Thanks again Charlie for doing this for us," Dan said as he folded up his receipt and paperwork for the boat rental and left the office.

CHAPTER 16

Charlene

Charlene found herself standing with the tab sheet in hand and thinking it odd that Joe didn't say anything about needing fishing line. It didn't really matter, she knew. He would never take advantage and would pay her. She could always trust Joe.

In the first year Charlene bought the resort she had been looking for someone she could rely on to fix the boat motors and take care of the water pumps and any other small engines. She looked in the phone book and saw the ad,

"It isn't dead until I say so."
McFadden small engine and boat motor
Repairs and maintenance
"Bringing back the SPARK"
705-861-7900

Charlene couldn't believe it. Could this be Joe McFadden? It had to be. Knowing Joe as she did, the words in the ad could only be his. She made the phone call and it was answered by a man with a Scottish accent, belonging to the man she knew had come to Canada from Scotland when he was 18-years-old to become a student at McMaster University in Hamilton.

She said, "Hi. Joe?"

The long silence that followed hit Charlene so viscerally she thought she would drop the phone. She was glad she didn't though, because when she knew he recognized her voice as well, and the way he said "Hello Charlene" the 10 years that passed since they last saw each other no longer mattered. It seemed like it was just yesterday when they looked at each other over the dead body on the autopsy table.

CHAPTER 17

Wednesday September 23rd, 2015

Bob

He watched Charlie through the binoculars as she stood on the dock holding the pontoon boat by the rails close to the dock so the students could get on. He saw the professor get in a fishing boat and start it up and just one pull. Maybe he would replace his motor with a nice new 9.9 hp Yamaha like the ones on all of Charlie's boats. It sounded smooth and didn't seem to cough or make faltering sounds like his motor did. He liked to watch her show guests how to work the little motor when they rented the boats from her. It even looked like the old lady in cottage #5 could start the motor easily. Maybe when I'm 65, he thought and the government could pay for it.

He thought Charlie, no Charlene, if that's what she prefers to be called, would be tired today. He heard the pontoon boat go over to the landing about 11:00 o'clock last night and heard laughter and loud talking on the way back. That wasn't right. They shouldn't make her stay up so late and have to boat over in the dark. Where were the girls? he thought, as he noticed only the three guys on the boat.

CHAPTER 18

Dan

"Just leave them," Dan yelled at the guys over the boat motors. "If they're too sick after a night at the pub to get out in the field today then they lose out. I don't want to keep Charlie waiting. Just get on the boat."

Greg told him at breakfast that he was over at the girls' cottage earlier and they were both still in bed. He said Lori said she felt a flu coming on and Ashley said she might be getting sick too. Dan believed Lori, but thought for sure that Ashley was just hung over. She had even more to drink at the Black Cat then he'd ever seen her drink at any university pub night. She was punching them back, and not just beer, she was into shots as well. Too bad there was no chance to talk to her without anyone overhearing.

He remembered that he saw Ashley and Haiden huddled in the pub hallway going to the bathrooms. When he walked by he overheard part of what they said. He heard Haiden say "What an old pervert" or something like that, and then he saw Haiden try to put his arms around Ashley. He watched her push him off and heard her say "You're the pervert!" before walking back toward the table with the rest of the group. Well not all them. Lori left their table after she and Greg seemed to be having words, too quietly for him to overhear with the din of the busy pub. She was the smartest of the group and perhaps she was losing patience with Greg who always seemed to be asking her questions about the assignments.

Greg seemed sullen for the rest of the night as Lori moved to stand at the bar beside some local yokel. They seemed to be hitting it off, so she stayed there the rest of the night and seemed reluctant to leave him when it was time to head back to be in time to meet Charlie at the dock.

Lori looked different he noticed. He was used to seeing her with her hair pulled back tight into a bun. When outside she always wore one of those funky caps, the kind that reminded Dan of a seafarer's hat with the little brim. Last night though, she wore her hair loose, and the curls flowed around her shoulders and the lights over the bar highlighted the brilliant red/orange colour. She had on a funky pair of glasses. She must wear contacts when outside and in class, because he couldn't remember seeing her wear them before. She looked radiant though, as she sipped on what looked like just water with lemon, laughing and flirting with the guy beside her.

Ashley just looked drunk, her long hair hung without shape or shine over her eyes. He wondered what he ever saw in her.

CHAPTER 19

Charlene

"Hi Sam. How are you today?" Charlene asked, as she veered the boat to the dock where Sam stood quietly waiting.

"Okay. Windy eh?" he said in a quiet flat tone in which he said everything it seemed to Charlene.

"Yes it is. I hope it calms down so you can get up the ladder and paint the trim on cottage #4 today," said Charlene. "I have to go into town soon so I won't be around to catch you when you get blown off. If you need first aid, I guess you'll have to get in a boat and drive it over here and drive to help."

Charlene knew Sam would be okay. She was just trying to get a rise out of him and see him smile. It seemed he never did. He was handsome though. At 26 he was in shape and clothes fit his strong-looking body well. He was just under 6' tall, clean-shaven, with his black hair pulled into a single braid that hung half-way down his back, Charlene knew he would have a killer smile, and be a great catch for any young woman. He told her more than once, though, that not many women are interested in a long term relationship with a single Dad of two girls under five-years-old.

She knew he would prop the tall extension ladder against the cottage built into a steep hill, and level it with a layer of rocks or logs. He could carry a paint can, brush, and rag up the ladder with one hand, cigarette in the other, and practically run up and down the ladder, no matter how high. He told her he wasn't nervous about heights at all and made some comment about working in New York on high rise structures as his other job.

She was too nervous to tackle the high parts of the cottages herself. She had Sam now to paint the high window frames and stain the top sections of the log frame cottages. He was also good with the ATV and trailer. He came in the fall for a few weeks to head into the back woods to drop some trees to season and to cut up the dead fall to have on hand for the cool fall and spring days. Charlene had him just dump the wood beside the shed. She liked the work of the chopping and piling the smaller pieces according to dryness and size, kindling or real fire burners in the wood stove.

She better top up the box of logs in the front porch of cottage #1 and take the wheelbarrow of punky wood for the students' outside fire pit. Otherwise they would burn the good wood meant for inside.

She also better get moving so she would make her appointment, which was really just an appointment to get her hair cut then go to the library to get more books before going to Joe's house for a late lunch, and hopefully some dessert, and not the kind that would add inches to her hips.

She had everything all planned and didn't want to change things so the professor could be picked up at the dock just to head out again in the fishing boat. It's better he has the boat now anyway, she thought. He can come and go as he pleases.

CHAPTER 20

Bob

He watched Charlene cross the lake earlier and heard her car leave the lot. He could see Sam putting the ladder up on the far side of cottage #4. Maybe he should get him to do some staining for him while it is still sunny and warm enough before winter. He noticed the wall that faced the spot where he parked his car looked dull and flaky against the bright red of his little Elantra, bought new with his work buy-out money. He meant to stain the cottage last summer. The previous owner hadn't touched the outside with a brush for many years. That could wait for later though. He needed to get ready.

He got his fishing rod already threaded with the new line he bought, and took everything down to the fishing boat. He noticed the rope on the boat and it reminded him of shopping he had to do next time in Espanola. He made sure there was plenty of fishing line left in the tackle box.

He heard the motor first then saw the professor dock the fishing boat at the resort and walk up the stairs to cottage #2.

CHAPTER 21

Dan

He motored the boat slowly along the shore of the lake. What was he thinking? Christ he was way too old to be with a woman Ashley's age. He could just imagine having to put up with all the shit that would come with the whole "more about me" time when she was in her 30s and 40s and then the menopause years, years when he watched his ex change into an angry bitch, always too hot or too cold, taking on an aggressive demeanour that scared him most of the time, and spending more time on activities that didn't include him. He didn't think he could take much more of it and was ready to call it quits. She didn't either apparently, since she left him while he was in class. He came home and she was gone, probably off to some yoga retreat with a bunch of other women in their late 50s.

He was still bitter that she left him, not giving him the pleasure of being the one to end it. He had his whole speech planned out and it still sat in his head with no opportunity to come out. He found himself saying it over and over to himself when he was stressed, like now.

She left most of their furniture though, surprised that she left her antique desk, but not surprised that she left a sheet of paper on top of it with her lawyer's information and her demands. She was always organized. He met her demands but only because after consulting a lawyer he realized he would be harder hit if she took him to court. She couldn't touch the small inheritance he got when his Dad died last year, his emergency stash. Depending on how things went today, Dan thought, he may have to dip into that fund himself and go away for a while. His attention was drawn back to the front of the boat.

CHAPTER 22

Charlene

She saw the girls in front of their cottage when she got back from town earlier than planned. The lunch date didn't take place, since Joe said he was working at fixing a motor for a young guy from town who was anxious to get out on the lake fishing as soon as possible. Charlene didn't mind. No, she did mind, but couldn't complain and wasn't mad at Joe. He phoned her cell while she was in town so she had lots of notice. Usually it was her job that prevented them from spending more time together.

Lori waved to her from the steps as she went up into the cottage. Ashley waved to her too as she walked away from Lori and walked to the back of the cottage.

It looked to Charlene like Ashley was heading for the trail system that Charlene marked along the deer run in the 50 acres behind the resort. She didn't look sick, at least not from that distance, she thought, as she watched her hike with strong strides to the woods. What were the girls playing at? she wondered. Oh, well, not her problem. With no date with Joe, and Dan and the Porters out on the lake with their own boat to get to their cars if needed, Charlene could get to work in the back bush marking trees for Sam to cut down in the next few weeks. She also had a mess to clean up at the shed behind the house along the tree line, where Sam helped her tear off old roofing shingles and replace them. She might as well get to it before winter so she wouldn't have to do it in the spring. Besides, it was a warm sunny day and she wanted to be outside. At some point she better go see how Sam was coming along with the painting.

CHAPTER 23

Bob

He saw two people in a fishing boat in the bay down the lake a bit close to the little island that was crown land. It looked like they had a fishing line in and must have anchored since the boat wasn't moving too much. The motor wasn't going anyway. He hoped they weren't going to pull up on shore since that's what he had in mind and didn't want anyone around.

CHAPTER 24

Dan

Now who is that? Dan wondered as he heard the motor of
another boat. He was hoping to be in a secluded part of the
lake. By the time he turned his head he missed the boat as it
went past him on the other side of the island. It sounded like
whoever it was slowed down then sped up again in a hurry.

CHAPTER 25

Charlene

It was too windy for Sam to finish the painting. He asked if it was okay with Charlene if he could just head home and catch up on some chores while the kids were in school. Charlene found Sam acting a little strange and was avoiding eye contact more than usual when they walked down to the pontoon boat so she could take him over to his car.

"What's up Sam?" she asked when they got to the landing. "Are you thinking you've had enough painting and don't want to come back?"

"Sam?" She tried to get his attention again. "I won't be offended. I hate all the painting too."

Sam looked at her for a long time before he said, "I'm not sure how to tell you this Charlie."

"What Sam?"

"It's only because I would want to know if it was me," he said.

"What! What!"

"I was up on the ladder painting when I heard a motor and

turned to look. I saw a guy in a fishing boat with a woman sitting up front. They were towing a kayak, a yellow kayak. Like you and Joe have. It was Joe. They were heading down the lake," he said not looking at Charlene.

"Are you sure it was Joe? Did you see him?" Charlene asked her stomach already in a knot.

"No," he said.

Phew. It could have been anyone she thought. It seemed everyone had yellow kayaks on the lake.

"It was too far. It had to be Joe's boat, the motor was making the same noises Joe's motor makes. You know that catchy sound like it's going to cut out and then revs up. The sound that drives you crazy because he hasn't fixed it yet since he's too busy fixing other people's motors," Sam explained.

"Could you see who was with him?" Charlene asked, not really wanting to know, but wanting to know more.

"No, I just saw long hair blowing back," he said.

"Thanks for telling me Sam. I'll see you later." It was all she could get out as Sam walked off the boat.

No, no, no, no! She couldn't believe Joe would do that to her! No wonder he canceled lunch. No! Even though she thought there must be some explanation she took the boat back over to the resort with a heavy heart.

CHAPTER 26

Bob

He felt fantastic. It had been building up inside him and the release was amazing.

He couldn't wait to download the photos. He was about to dock and get at it when he saw the van at the resort landing. The students were back. He looked at his watch. It was only 3:30 p.m. He wondered why they were so early. He took his boat over to the dock, if only to prolong the way he felt. They told him they finished early and were just about to pick up the phone to call Charlene to come and get them. He said he would boat them over so Charlene wouldn't have to bother. They took him up on his offer and he let them off in front of cottage #1 before heading back across the lake to his cottage and his laptop.

CHAPTER 27

Dan

When the professor docked the boat and started to walk up to the office to tell Charlie he was back, he was surprised to see the guys back already and in front of the cottage, beer bottles lined up on the picnic table. Was it after 5:00 pm already? He barely had time to do what he needed to do. Wasn't that the Scottish canoe group coming out of the office? That seemed like a fast trip. He thought they were supposed to be gone another day.

He would wait until Charlie was finished checking the canoes over. Dan watched as she checked the inside and outside of the canoes before giving the group the thumbs up. They were all clearly in a good mood and looked like they spent a month in the bush and not just one night.

They couldn't have picked nicer fall days with temperatures going up to 20 degrees Celsius each day, and warmer out of the wind in the direct sun. The colours on the trees were magnificent against the robin-egg blue of the September sky. He heard one of the men ask Charlie if they could have a picnic in front of the beach to dry out before she took them back to their SUV parked at the landing. Charlie must have said yes because they walked over to the beach and stretched themselves out on the beach chairs facing the lake.

"Did something happen for them to come back early?" he asked Charlie as she was dragging a canoe back to the canoe rack. "Here, I'll give you a hand," he said, picking up the end of the canoe.

"No. They just had enough they said."

Charlie laughed and added, "One night with husbands and wives in the bush is usually enough for any couple."

"No, they seemed to be all still getting along. That wasn't nice of me to say that. I've got something unpleasant on my mind right now," she said thinking again of Joe.

"They are heading to Sudbury from here to visit the Big Nickle, then they will drive east. One of them has a daughter in Nova Scotia, going to St. Francis Xavier University. They are going to tour the area and drop off their car rental in Halifax and fly home from there."

"Don't you have family in Nova Scotia?" Dan asked, remembering something about an old house there or something.

"You have a good memory Dan! My grandfather's house was left to my father and his brothers. Nobody wanted it. They had it appraised and it went up for sale this past spring. I bought it for next to nothing. It's a fixer-upper. I'd been to Nova Scotia on driving trips a few times in the years before I bought the resort and drove by the house once. I don't remember anything about my visit there as a kid but I love the area. I hope to live in the house and work on it when the resort closes up for the season."

They worked together to get the three canoes upside down on the slots on the rack.

Charlie gave Dan a big smile when she noticed the students were back and she didn't have to pick them up, thinking Dan must have gone over in the fishing boat when she was in the back bush. She would have been ready to pick them up, but it was nice to keep working while it was such a nice day.

"That's odd," Charlie said when they had the last canoe on the rack. "Someone's moved my kayak.

She walked over to the kayak to the side of the rack closest to the shore. She pushed some branches aside and put her hands on top of the kayak.

"It's wet," she said. She pulled at a piece of weed stuck on the handle at the end of the kayak.

"It's turned the wrong way on the rack too. I always store it so the back goes in first so the seat can fold down into the kayak as I push it back on the rack. And it's on the first tier instead of the second," she added.

Dan looked at Greg, who looked right at him before turning his back to face Peter.

"I never put it here. I don't like this spot," said Charlie. "It's too close to the brush and water snakes."

She turned to the students and asked if they took the kayak out.

"No. I didn't," said Peter.

"Nope," said Haiden.

Greg took longer to answer, almost like he didn't hear

Charlie, Dan thought.

"No," he finally said.

Charlie started to drag the kayak off the rack. Dan moved to the back of the rack. They both took an end. Dan pushed and Charlie pulled.

"God it's heavy," said Dan.

"It feels like it's full of water, but nothing's coming out," said Charlie.

"Hold on Dan. I better check what's going on."

Dan watched Charlie crawl over the wooden beams of the rack. She stepped one foot into the water at the shore then got down on her hands and knees. He noticed she had on her high green rubber boots, the kind the Queen wore, she once told him.

"Aaahhh no," said Charlie quietly as she looked into the kayak from below. "Don't push Dan. We need to leave the kayak right where it is."

"Why. What's wrong?" he asked as he ducked under the rack, crawled to the side of the kayak and turned his head to look up. He turned to face Charlie. They looked at one another before he backed up, walked around the rack and stood waiting while Charlie crawled back out to join him.

CHAPTER 28

Charlene

The O.P.P. officer docked the police boat in front of cottage #3 after Charlene waved him away from the dock in front of cottage #1. He looked puzzled, but followed Charlene's frantic hand gestures and did what he was told.

"Hi James. I'm not sorry to see you again, but I am sorry it's under these circumstances. How have you been?" Charlene greeted the young police officer as she caught the line he threw to her to tie the boat to the dock. "I guess it's just you. No new officers hired yet?"

"Hey Ms. Parker," he said. "It's great to see you again. You're stuck with me until Sarah shows up. She was off today but at home, so she should be here as soon as she goes to the station and gets her gear. I haven't seen you for months and now I've seen you twice in one day! I saw you in town earlier as you were pulling out from the side street. More books eh? I wish I had time to read." His smirk told Charlene he was trying to get a rise out of her, knowing how busy she was too.

"I wish you would just call me Charlene," she said, again, thinking it unlikely that would ever happen. He kept himself in his Officer James Edwards role, and was formal when he was on the job and off the job, with her anyway.

"I was on my way to a fender bender on the highway so couldn't stop to chat. I was just finishing up that report and eating my lunch when dispatch sent me here. It was lucky the boat was at the station and all set to hook up," he said, as he ignored what Charlene just said to him.

"I knew you would be here all night and I have guests to take care of, so I won't be at your beck and call with the pontoon boat. I was up late last night with the students and now this. I doubt I will get much sleep anyway," said Charlene as they walked off the dock toward cottage #1, where she noticed Dan standing inside the screen porch watching them. He backed into the shadow when he saw her look over.

"I have the geology students here and that's Professor Dan Bowen," whispered Charlene. "He was with me at the canoe rack. I told him to go inside the cottage with the students. The three guys went inside as we were trying to move the kayak, so I don't know what they saw or heard. There are two other students, both girls."

She and the officer looked at each other without saying anything.

"They're staying in cottage #2. I told Dan to keep quiet and not say anything to the students until you arrived. He was inside the cottage when I called 9-1-1. I had my cell on me and managed to get a signal. I tried to keep my voice down when I talked to the dispatcher. I had a bit of trouble explaining the boat situation since they are in North Bay, and probably don't know much about this area. She was good though, not panicky," Charlene said as she steered him toward the canoe rack.

She put her arm out to the side to stop him as he seemed intent on walking right into the crime scene.

"That's why I had you dock in front of #3. This whole area may be your scene," Charlene was careful to say 'may' and guide him rather than tell him what to do.

She met Officer Edwards three years ago when he started his policing career and she needed some help from the police to escort a drunken couple off the resort. Both the husband and wife started drinking as she picked them up on the pontoon boat, and didn't stop for the first three days of their week-long stay. She had to talk to them about their loud voices after the 11:00 pm quiet time on the first night and then she had to talk to them and warn them about loud swearing during the day. Their cottage was right in front of the beach and the other guests didn't like what their kids were hearing. She had to take the fishing boat they rented away from their dock since they were drunk most of the time. That led to a heated discussion in the office about wanting money back and demanding the right to use the boat. Charlene pointed to the paperwork they signed that included the right to forfeit the use of the boat and then warned them they would be asked to leave the resort if they didn't change their behaviour. They seemed to get the picture. But later the husband started calling up to Charlene as she was in the kitchen after the office closed. She told him she would call the police and have them removed as trespassers, but that didn't seem to bother him. He kept calling her name, not saying much more, but clearly still drunk. The other guests seemed amused but Charlene was not.

Officer Edwards and another young officer arrived and waited patiently while the couple packed up their belongings The couple were submissive once they saw the police officers walk up to their cottage. Charlene took them all back to the landing. They were both too drunk to drive, so the officers drove them to Espanola to a motel then drove them back the next day so they could get their car and leave.

James was stationed just outside of Espanola and really seemed to fit in with the community. He was only 24-years-old but got along well with everyone. He grew up with Sam on the same Anishinaabe Indian reservation, and Sam told her James was a great liaison with the first nation police on site there. It also didn't hurt that he was fit and handsome, with short black hair, and dimples in both cheeks when he smiled. More importantly though, he treated everyone with great respect on or off the job, especially his elders, like her, Charlene thought, thinking he could easily be her son.

He was a real homebody, and only left the area for the time it took to go to training at the police college in Aylmer. The last time Charlene saw him, James told her he moved out of his parents' home and moved in with his girlfriend Tracy, into a reserve house on the same street. He once told her Tracy was not a good cook so he wanted to be close enough to pop in to eat his Mom's home-cooked meals. He had to do it on the sly though he told her, being careful not to hurt Tracy's feelings. He often stopped in to visit Charlene at lunch time in the fall or spring, not adverse to home-made macaroni and cheese, or a biscuit or four with a big bowl of her home-made soup.

Charlene liked how he handled himself on the trespass call, quiet and polite. She worked with him on another police matter after that and got to know him a fair bit. She knew though, that his enthusiasm did not match his experience. He needed guidance in criminal investigations, like not walking onto a crime scene.

Focusing back on this police matter, as soon as she saw the body Charlene got right into police mode. As a former detective with the Hamilton Police Service, she knew she had to take care not to disturb the area as much as possible. She and Professor Bowen had already walked and crawled around the canoe rack. There was not much to be done about that. While waiting for the police to arrive she got the tarp from the pontoon boat storage bench and spread it out under the kayak, trying to put her feet into the same place where she had stepped before. She marked her passage with small sticks she picked up along the path along the shore. She asked the professor to remove his hikers and leave them upside down on newspaper on the porch. The police would want to check his boot tread against any footprints they found around the kayak. She saw that he changed into Crocs as he came out to tell her the boots were available if need be. He went back into the cottage. She knew she should take her rubber boots off too, but she didn't trust leaving the site, so she didn't.

She noticed there were drips of moisture coming from the

kayak to the ground below. The tarp would protect the ground below it and catch what was falling from above. It looked like water. She wasn't sure if she should put another tarp over the second level of the rack to protect the kayak below. There were canoes on the third level and Charlene was worried she may disturb insects or leaves or whatever had naturally gathered in the underside of the canoes. She decided she should leave it alone.

She was careful to watch cottage #1 making sure no one came out and no one went near the canoe rack. At this stage, everyone on the resort would be treated as a suspect, including her.

"I like your crime scene tape Ms. Parker," Officer Edwards said with only a bit of a smile, always careful it seemed to Charlene not to offend, but to add some levity to a terrible situation. Like most officers Charlene met, that was one way of dealing with what they experienced as part of their job.

Charlene collected some yellow rope from the shed when she got the tarp. She used the rope for makeshift clotheslines between trees for guests who wanted to hang up wet bathing suits and towels. Now though, she strung the rope from the side of the canoe rack closest to cottage #1 and attached it at the other end to the picnic table in front of the cottage. She tried to rope off as much of the scene as she could, knowing it was likely not big enough, but with all the bush and shoreline around, the suspect could have come and gone from all different places. She tied bits of fluorescent trail tape at intervals so no one would walk into the rope in the dark, which was coming in fast.

It would be pitch black by 8:15 or 8:30 pm this time of year, the first day of fall, Charlene just read in the Farmer's Almanac earlier that day. She liked to have the quirky books in each of the rental cottages as well, so the guests who were as interested as she was, could find out when the sun was expected to rise and set, and the best times to fish, etc. There were lots of good recipes in the books as well, and Charlene would try most of them after the resort was closed when she would have more time to slow cook in the kitchen.

It's too bad this has happened, she thought, the police would have lights set up around the canoe rack. If the lights were still up, she may not see the total eclipse of the moon that was going to happen in a few days, hopefully visible from the sky above the resort. She planned to sit on a dock and watch.

She shook her head, upset with herself at thinking of the moon at a time like this. It was her way too when she was a police officer and had to see sights that no one wanted to see. She found if she didn't think too much about what she was seeing and doing, the details could be brought to mind if needed, but she could protect herself from the stress. Some officers liked to talk about every case that was upsetting, but Charlene preferred to sort it out in her mind and file it and not allow it to get in her way of the positive things in her life.

She thought back to an especially gruesome shift when she arrived at work on December 31st, and was met by the day shift detective who told her to hurry and get her gear, they had a suspicious death to investigate. They drove together to a nice little house in the subdivision on the mountain above Hamilton. Firefighters were on scene, putting the hoses back onto the truck. The captain walked over to their car, his eyes revealing what they hadn't yet seen. He told them they were finished and were awaiting direction from the Fire Marshall who was on his way to the scene.

Charlene and Derek walked up to the house, obviously the one they were to go to with the burnt attached garage to the left. The garage door was down. They walked up to the door and rang the bell, respecting the owner's privacy, even though patrol officers and firefighters had been all over the house by now. The door was opened by the beat officer. A volunteer with the Victim Services group was already there and introduced herself. She sat beside a woman in her mid-thirties, who was crying and rocking herself on the ottoman in front of an easy chair that had a book and eyeglasses on the seat. Charlene remembered thinking it was unlikely the book would be picked up for some time.

The woman told them, between her sob bursts, that she drove home from work that day, pulled into the driveway, unlocked the front door, and walked into her foyer filled with smoke. Seeing soot at the bottom of the door in the hallway leading to the garage she opened the door, then closed it and phoned 9-1-1. Firefighters and police were there within minutes and though the fire was mostly out, the woman had much, much more to deal with. She explained she saw her ex-boyfriend's car in the garage engulfed in smoke and small areas of fire. She said she caught a glimpse of her boyfriend sitting behind the wheel of his car. She could only see his teeth and the whites of his dead eyes against the charred black of his body. She managed to close the door before she dialed for help and sat on the ottoman until help arrived. She said she wondered why she didn't fear the smoke or fire and leave the house. Charlene thought it was likely as far as the adrenaline would carry her legs before she collapsed. She also thought it would be likely the woman would have many sleepless nights or bad dreams recalling the horrible scene and gruesome death.

As she told her story, Charlene and Derek learned that the woman had broken off the relationship just a week before he set his body on fire in her garage. She said her two young children did not like him and she wasn't ready to be with someone her kids were not comfortable with. She didn't like his mood swings either and told him she was not ready to take on the relationship any longer. He began phoning her and phoned every day about 10 times. She said she was just about to pick up rather than let the phone ring, and tell him she would report him to police if he did not stop calling. No one had to say it was too late for that, but they were all thinking it.

Charlene took her statement as Derek made a call to his wife on his cell phone to say he would be late for their New Year's Eve party. It was 6:00 pm and his shift ended at 4:30 pm when Charlene's shift started. Charlene overheard him, but tried to concentrate on what the woman was telling her. The fire captain came in and Derek put his phone away and went out with him. Charlene knew there would be time to get a more detailed statement, but she also knew that the woman may have set the fire and was a suspect, so she had to pay close attention to whatever clues were evolving. She also had to get into the garage and view the scene and the deceased, knowing clues would abound there too. She left the woman with the volunteer and patrol officer and checked with the firefighters to see if she could enter the garage safely. She could and she did, with the Fire Marshall, who had just arrived.

What remained of the ex-boyfriend was a skeleton, sitting mostly upright in the driver's seat staring at nothing through the windshield. His eyes were wide open, all the skin black and burned around them. His teeth looked like they were set in a crazy smile, so white in contrast to all the burnt skin of his face and neck. His arms were bent at the elbow and his hands were up close to the steering wheel, burnt and still in a position as though he had his hands on the wheel, but moved them as the wheel burned and the flames went from the interior of the car up the steering wheel then up his arms. He could have been alive while on fire when he moved his hands off the wheel. She hoped he was already dead though, his arms moving off the wheel as they burned. The Fire Marshall would investigate that. He did say that the way the windows were only partially open, would indicate the deceased or whoever started the fire knew the draft would accelerate the flames making for a vicious yet quick burn. Both front windows were open slightly and the back windows closed.

A Tim Horton's cup, half-filled with milky-looking liquid sat in the cup holder beside him. Inside the car there was a strong gasoline smell among the acrid smoke. Charlene knew she would have to shower, wash her hair and change her suit once she got back to the station. She brought the lapel of her coat over her nose and mouth and got as close to the body as she was allowed. She called dispatch to see if anyone from the Major Crimes Unit, more experienced than they were, could come to the scene or advise them as to what they should do. No one was answering their phones though, as usual it seemed. The police service was understaffed and everyone was always busy. She and Derek made the decision themselves to seize the Tim Horton's cup as possible evidence, a drugging perhaps, and to leave the body in the car and have the whole car towed to the garage of the morgue. The coroner had been notified and was satisfied with that decision. He would view the body in the car in the garage in the basement of the hospital downtown Hamilton, before moving him to the morgue inside.

Derek said he would drive the unmarked police car while Charlene went in the tow truck to the morgue ensuring continuity of any evidence on the body and in the car. Once they both arrived, they had a quick chat with the pathologist, and began the tedious task of filing reports in the office to the side of the examination room.

After putting on gloves again, they went into the examination room where the body had been moved, to check his pockets for identification. Charlene had already called for an officer from the Identification Branch to come and try for fingerprints as well. A wallet was in his back pocket with a driver's licence that was surprisingly still legible. Charlene had an address to check for next of kin that matched the address assigned to his car registration. A Scene of Crime Officer, known as a SOCO officer, trained in fingerprinting, as well as any evidence collection, arrived and was able to get a print for comparison with any known print on police file. It wasn't easy for him though, the skin of the fingers and hands were so burnt through so many layers, the skin slipped off like gloves. The skin was bagged in an evidence bag and they covered his hands in bags to protect them until the autopsy. They sealed the drawer with police tape after the body was placed inside and contacted the Major Crimes Unit again, to make them aware of the situation. They had to leave a phone message, but knew their reports would make it on the Staff Sergeant's desk by the next shift as well as be taken over to the Major Crimes Unit later that shift, so everyone would know what was going on with the deceased and the investigation so far.

She checked her watch and told Derek she would take over by herself at that point so he could make his party and see in the New Year with his wife. He had already worked a long day and it wouldn't take two of them to contact the next of kin and do the reports. A decision she later regretted making. She drove him back to the station so he could get his car. He would be in the next day anyway and could file his reports then.

Charlene drove to the deceased's address and the apartment door was opened by a beautiful, black woman dressed in colourful clothes and lots of gold jewellery. They had asked the woman at the scene of the fire what colour her boyfriend's skin was before the fire. It wouldn't be the first time a victim of fire was not the person the police were told it was. Even though it was her boyfriend's car, it could have been any man sitting dead inside it. There was no way of recognizing facial features after a fire like that. They were told he was white.

The woman in the apartment was the deceased's wife, not aware her husband had been cheating on her. She had that to digest as well as the fact that he was dead. They had a young daughter, just a toddler, asleep in her room. Charlene phoned the woman's sister to come for support. No one was available from Victim Services, being New Year's Eve they were lucky to have the woman at the house with the woman who discovered his body.

After taking a statement from the deceased's wife, and staying until the sister arrived from across the city, Charlene went back to the station to write the reports. She knew she would be back at work the next day, but she needed the reports to be as complete as possible before she could go home. She had to put the various copies in trays to go to Records Branch, Identification Branch, Major Crimes Unit, as well as on her own boss's desk. She smelled of smoke and despair. The wife had been despondent and her angst was soaked into Charlene as though Charlene was a sponge. The whole ordeal so far had permeated her whole being. She recalled her saying again and again how her husband just bought her a beautiful watch for Christmas. She showed it to Charlene over and over again, as if to prove that he loved her and couldn't be dead in another woman's garage. Charlene couldn't bear to tell her that her husband was on file on a charge of sexual assault against a young person, but, of course, she had to considering their child asleep in the next room. Charlene discovered this when she dropped Derek off at the station. She called Records Branch to see if she could get more information about the deceased before heading to his apartment, and discovered the pending charge with a court date coming soon.

Somehow the knowledge of the allegation of the sexual

assault and a prior conviction for sexual assault made Charlene not feel so bad that he was dead. It made her really angry thinking of how selfish he was to have set himself on fire in his former girlfriend's house, if that's what happened, and cheating on his wife to boot, never mind his poor assault victims. It was difficult to watch his wife cry and deny that he would ever cheat or be in trouble with police. It seemed he kept his cheating, criminal conviction and new charge from her, keeping her in the dark as to the kind of man he really was. She remembered that she seemed more upset about the cheating and didn't really hear, or wouldn't, or couldn't, also take in the criminal matters. Her mind must have been in overload hearing everything from Charlene like that.

Copies of the reports would have to be sent to central station to the Child Abuse Branch so the investigating detective could notify the Court Branch that the deceased would not be making his court appearance. There would be no justice for the victim or her family now. They would not see their day in court. What a mess, she remembered thinking about that night. She thought back to when she was at her desk writing the reports when she heard the announcer on the police station radio say that it was a new year. She looked at her watch, getting frantic and frustrated with how late it was and how little she felt she had accomplished so far into her shift. She had so much more to do, but felt she couldn't focus. Had she even eaten? No, she realized her last meal was at noon at home.

She picked up the phone and called her parents, not caring about the no personal calls rule for long distance. When her

Mom answered, Charlene couldn't talk for a few minutes. When she could, she told her mother she was having a terrible shift at work and just wanted to say she loved her and to wish her a happy new year. She could barely keep the crack out of her voice when she said she was okay in response to her mother's concerned questions and said goodbye, not being able to stop the tears that rolled down her cheeks onto the desk.

Charlene thought how selfish it must have been to call, crack up, and say good bye, worrying her parents like that, but that's what she did without thinking.

She brought her mind back to the present and saw Officer Edwards examining the outside area beyond her yellow roped area.

Having finished their picnic and seeing the police boat come to the dock seemed to pique the curiosity of the canoeists. They sauntered over to say they were ready to go across to their car. Charlene was sure they really wanted to see an Ontario police officer up close, but then she checked her watch and realized an hour had passed from the time she called 9-1-1 and Officer Edwards arrived so the group was probably anxious to get on the road.

Charlene introduced them to Officer Edwards, and told him the group had returned to the resort prior to the discovery. He took the hint and asked if they would wait in the office for a few minutes until he could come and speak to them before they left. He told them he would explain as soon as he could.

As they walked away following his request, he said, "I better wait for Sarah before I let them leave Ms. Parker. Are they okay in the office? I guess I should have asked you first," he added.

"That was a great idea James. I think that's the best place for them. It's getting damp and dark, and I got the wood stove going just before they came back. It will be cozy for them in there. They were all sitting by the beach so they don't know what's happening, but they'll be expecting to head out soon though. They told me they wanted to get to Sudbury tonight. It's only an hour drive, but I think they're pooped from the canoe trip," Charlene explained.

"Where are they from?" Officer Edwards asked.

"Scotland," she told him.

"All the more reason to not trust them," he replied, rolling his eyes and smiling.

It was common knowledge in the area that many of the Anishinaabe living on James' reserve were descendants of the union between a Scottish fishing captain, Alexander MacGregor, and a native woman. The captain was a fisherman in the area in about 1850 and he married and settled in the area. He was buried near the river in the nearby village. The name was changed to McGregor over time and the bay was named after him.

Officer Edwards name was traced back to Wales and England and not Scotland, the non-native name given to his family years ago, but any Celtic name was fodder for his amusement. Charlene wondered if he would take on an aboriginal name at some time.

"What's the origin of your name Ms. Parker, if you don't mind me asking?"

"Scotland," she said smiling waiting for his reaction and getting it as he rolled his eyes again. "It means 'keeper of the park'"

"That's cool since you keep this land," he said.

"And I hope to keep it. If you lot will get on with this, I can get on with my business," she said, upset at her memories and the present situation.

CHAPTER 29

Charlene

The headlights could be seen across the water in the parking lot. Charlene told Officer Edwards she would go over with the pontoon boat. He said he would take the police boat, but Charlene suggested he may want to keep an eye on the crime scene. He had the knowledge to blush slightly before thanking her from letting him make a big mistake. She also told him before she left that the Porters were in cottage #5 and they were the only other guests at the resort. She said she heard the motor of their rental boat, then saw the boat tied to the dock just before she started to drag the canoes back to the rack. She hadn't heard it leave again so figured they were inside the cottage for the night.

"Okay, more witnesses to be interviewed. Gotcha. I'll let Sarah know," he said.

Charlene took the big flashlight with her, knowing the parking lot light did not light up the entire dock. She pulled on the lights on the pontoon boat, and carefully made her way to the landing. When she arrived, O.P.P. Detective Sarah

Davidson was waiting with the coroner on the dock, ready to hop on the boat.

"Hi Sarah," said Charlene.

"Oh man Staff. I'm sorry. What are you, a magnet for dead bodies?"

Charlene knew that Sarah also used black humour as her way of having to deal with dismal and dire situations, and being the only major crime detective in the area, she had to investigate most of them. Sometimes the local O.P.P. station had to call in help from Sudbury, but Sarah hated when that happened. She liked to be in charge and didn't like other detectives trying to take over her cases. Sarah told Charlene she didn't really like many of the male officers working in major crimes. Though she was out, she still put up with jokes and jeers from the guys trying to get her to switch teams. Sarah lived with a woman 10 years her senior in a house on a large lot just off Highway 17. The location was good for Sarah, just a five minute drive to the police station, and Patty, her partner, had plenty of room to park her semi and hit the road four days a week for a local trucking company. Sarah took advantage of the days when Patty was on the road and spent most of her time at the police station, so they could have some time together when Patty came home.

Sarah was referring to the case last summer when Charlene found a dead man hanging from a tree. She was returning from taking cottagers from the parking lot to their cottage. Each year she took the woman and her elderly mother, both from Tennessee, to their old family cottage on one of the islands at the start of the season and brought them back at the end of the summer. They kept their boat on shore at the cottage and needed a ride to get there. They were regular customers of Charlene's, getting gas for the boat, ice for an old fridge they used more as a cooler, and propane tanks. There was no hydro out there and they used propane lights inside the cottage.

At the end of the season they would bring Charlene a box of cake mix and frosting, a can of pineapples, and a jar of maraschino cherries, thinking Charlene would make some sort of upside down cake. Little did they know she just ate the cherries dipped in the icing and put the cake mix in the kitchen cupboard, where she now had three boxes stored, awaiting some sort of boxed cake emergency. Charlene preferred to bake from scratch. The pineapples she just ate in a bowl whenever she had a hankering for something sweet.

Last year, after she dropped the women off, Charlene took the boat around the back side of their island and saw the body hanging among the leaves. Sarah was the detective on that case. Though more than 10 years younger than Charlene, they hit it off and Sarah called her Staff, after she learned Charlene had been a former police detective with the rank of Staff Sergeant. Though Charlene was qualified as an Inspector after passing her exams, she didn't get promoted to that rank before she quit the police service and started her new life. She often reminded Sarah that she once outranked Sarah's sergeant rank, and the two of them had fun with that each time they saw each other. Charlene often dropped into the police station when she had more time during the off season just so she could visit with Sarah.

Charlene walked to the front of the boat and gave Sarah a big hug. She walked back to the motor controls and just before she put the boat into reverse, she acknowledged the coroner, standing quietly at the front of the boat, medical bag in hand.

"Hello Joe," she said.

"Hello Charlene," he replied.

CHAPTER 30

Charlene

"Oh come off it and just give the man a big hug and kiss," said Sarah.

Charlene talked about Joe to Sarah often, and Sarah knew they were a couple. She also knew that both Joe and Charlene gave each other professional distance when they met on police matters, like the hanging. She liked to tease them both though and see if she could get them to crack.

Joe was a forensic pathologist and coroner, on contract with the local hospital for six months a year to attend sudden and suspicious deaths and guide the local O.P.P. officers through the ordeal following the finding of a deceased person. He was called by police, mandated by the provincial Coroner's Act, to investigate to identify the body, find out when the death occurred, where it happened, how it happened, and by what means, whether by homicide, accident, natural causes or by suicide like the hanging turned out to be. He directed the police officers to interview any potential witness, speak to family members, get medical information or whatever it took to find the answers. He also performed the autopsies, seeking the physical evidence to determine cause of death.

Joe spent the other six months on contract in Hamilton doing the same thing there in the fall and winter. He was the full time pathologist there before he made the move north to Georgian Bay. He started his engine repair business from a shed at his house set on a small peninsula on the big water, surrounded by water on three sides and a view out front of small islands dotting the shallow water.

It was something he always wanted to do, knowing that there would be some coroner-related work but not as much as in Hamilton. He told Charlene he wanted to work at taking something apart and be able to bring it back to life for a change. He always had an interest in engine repairs, but never had the time before he semi-retired. Charlene was glad he would not be renewing his Hamilton contract this fall. They could have a lot of time together when his engine business closed up for the winter and the resort shut down.

Charlene first met Joe when she was a new recruit with the regional police in Hamilton, fresh out of Aylmer Police College. She was in uniform patrol for about a week, when her sergeant told her to head to the Hamilton General Hospital to watch an autopsy. Several other male officers on her shift had never been to an autopsy before, so the four of them found themselves watching Dr. Joe McFadden start the bone saw and cut through the forehead of a man lying face-up on a stainless steel table after being found a few hours earlier, floating face-down in the harbour. Two of the men walked out at that point. The other man looked at Charlene, rolled his eyes, and lasted until Joe peeled the forehead and top of the man's head back took the brain out and put it on the weigh scale. The officer covered his mouth and leaned back against the wall on wobbly legs before he had the strength to run from the room.

"Well officer, I guess it's just you and me," Joe said to Charlene.

Though Charlene never got used to the smell of an autopsy, particularly when the Y incision was made to reveal the internal organs for examination, she never had to leave the room. She was fascinated by the science and the clues the body could give to the expert examiner, and she appreciated that Joe treated the body as a person, calling the deceased by name throughout the medical examination. She heard him speak sharply on many occasions to police officers or his own assistants who were not respectful in the presence of the person unfortunate enough to end up on his table being taken apart and examined. She also heard Joe speak to family members of the deceased and he was compassionate, sincere and caring, and timely with his reports that no matter how quick, was never soon enough for family needing and wanting answers.

That was part of what made her fall in love with him. The other parts fell into place about six years later when Charlene became a detective and suspicious deaths became a part of her normal shift. As part of her investigation, she had to attend all autopsies that concerned her cases. She felt comfortable being close to Joe and felt a spark that came with the attraction. Though for the most part she could only see Joe's eyes over the mask, she felt she got to know his moods and she felt she shared in his discoveries just by watching his pale blue eyes as they searched and tracked and stored what he was seeing on the body on the table. He looked up often and looked into the light gray of Charlene's eyes, and the crinkles at the sides of his eyes grew deeper, as his eyes smiled at hers.

He was the pathologist on duty that New Year's Eve night. She could still bring to mind the way he looked at her, pulled down his mask, walked over, and gave her a kiss and said, 'Happy New Year ahead of time Charlene' before getting back to the burnt body. She thought then that he felt the same way about her, but Charlene was married at the time and so was Joe. They never met in any social setting other than over coffee at his desk as they discussed a case.

Then Charlene was no longer married, having divorced when she turned 45-years-old. She focused her attention on her cases and spent more time working then playing, and lasted another four years before she realized she was aging too fast with the stress and quit her job. She traveled for a year then bought Kirk Lake Camp when she turned 50, spending some of her hard earned money, and money from the sale of her house in a small village outside of Hamilton.

She wasn't too worried about the six-cottage seasonal business. One of the guests from Germany, who came with his wife each July and stayed in the one-room cottage for a few weeks, said he would buy the resort anytime she wanted to sell. He was in love with the hilly land, the solitude of the location, and wanted to turn the resort into a private spot for his family and friends for the summer months only.

Charlene wasn't ready to sell yet though. Especially not since she made that phone call three years ago to McFadden's small engine repair and reconnected with Joe.

She lost touch with him after she was transferred to the Sexual Assault Unit and no longer investigated sudden deaths. She had no reason to be in contact with him but thought of him often and imagined his smiling eyes as she recovered from her separation and divorce and moved on in life. She found out when they met that same day after her phone call, he left his wife and they divorced just a year after she had. They began to see each other and the social occasions turned from dates to stay-overs, and a longing to see each other more often, still wanting their own lives, but getting closer to something more permanent, but not yet talking about it.

Charlene had hopes to spend months together this fall and winter, renovating the old family home she bought in the small harbour along the eastern shore. Now, what would happen? Who was that woman he was with on the boat? Why didn't he tell her? Fuck, she thought. This, and no time to talk to him with everyone around.

CHAPTER 31

Bob

He couldn't make anything out with the binoculars anymore, other than the brightly lit area around the canoe rack at the resort. He watched Charlie earlier, Charlene he corrected himself, talking to a police officer in front of cottage #1. There was rope all around. He missed that going up, he was so intent on looking at the pictures he downloaded to his computer.

He saw Joe and a woman wearing a suit jacket and slacks come over on the pontoon boat later with boxes of stuff, maybe the lights, he thought. She must be a police officer too, since he watched her walk around with authority and watched her point to the office before the uniformed officer walked up and went inside. He could just make out that people were inside with all the lights on. Not long after, he heard Charlene start up the pontoon boat and head to the landing. He could just make out that a group was on board. The police boat was still tied to the dock, so the officer must have stayed behind. This will get very interesting, he thought, as he got the bottle of Jim Beam down from the cupboard and settled on the couch for a long night, still excited and reliving the rush of the day.

CHAPTER 32

Charlene

"Can you stay James?" Sarah asked him as he took pictures of the canoe rack and kayak, still on the lower level, where Charlene left it. "You will be in for a long shift."

"And lots of overtime...I mean experience," he said looking aside at Charlene, rolling his eyes.

"I'm glad you were able to get what you needed from the canoeists and let them get going," Charlene told Sarah and James. "I don't think they had anything to do with this."

"No, I don't either Staff. James got their details and we'll know where they will be tonight. They gave us the hotel they booked and their itinerary for the next week and we can be in touch if needed. I'm glad you saw them paddle in, but they could have come to shore then gone out again, so we have to be careful we don't exclude them from the investigation," Sarah said.

"Or they may have seen something, they don't know is important to the investigation," Charlene offered.

"Yes. They were out on the water in the area so we will be

sure to get more detailed statements," Sarah said.

"I have Officer Miller on her way," she continued. "She came in for the night shift. Elliot Lake detachment said they would send an officer to our station to take any calls in our area, and Blind River will back up Elliot Lake, and, of course Espanola police will help us out too." Sarah explained to Officer Edwards and to Joe, who was on his back laying in the grass looking up under the kayak. He looked like a big bunny wearing a white one-piece forensic paper suit and shoe covers. The ears were missing from the hood though, and the mask over his face made him look ominous in the glare of the halogen lights. She looked down and saw that James and Sarah had their feet covered and were wearing gloves. Charlene stood back.

"Wow. I wouldn't want to be the person needing police help quickly tonight," Charlene said. Elliot Lake was about an hour from Espanola and Blind River 40 minutes west from Elliot Lake.

"We do what we can Staff, you know that. There is still one of ours left at the station too," Sarah said, defending her team.

"Well then, you're all set" Charlene said, looking aside at Officer Edwards and rolling her eyes for a change.

"Why don't you head in Staff and eat and get warm. You've done lots for us already," Sarah said seeing how tired Charlene looked.

"I think I will," she replied, thinking she would put a big pot of her leftover stew on the stove and make some buns in case anyone got hungry, which they would she knew.

Just as she turned to leave, Joe said, "Okay let's get the kayak out of here."

Charlene turned back and watched and waited.

Sarah and James zipped up their paper suits and covered their faces with masks before going to the rack to help Joe with the kayak. James went around to the end of the kayak close to the woods behind the rack. Joe had the end close to the picnic table in front of cottage #1. Sarah crawled to the side of the kayak and helped. They got the kayak off the rack, turned it over and moved it out onto the tarp they had spread out in readiness. Charlene stood rooted unable to turn away.

Once the kayak was on the centre of the tarp and the lights adjusted to spotlight it, they all stood and looked at it, then at each other. The woman had been stuffed, face up into the kayak. Charlene's black graphite paddle was on top of the her. Her hands were tied to each other with rope and then tied to the paddle, her hands resting at her groin. The paddle was set into the kayak on top of her, the blades under the rim of the opening in the kayak. It was what stopped her from falling out of the overturned kayak in the rack, thought Charlene.

The kayak seat was missing. Her head was pushed up under the rim of the kayak into the small storage space that was behind where the seat should be, so only her chin was visible. The swell of breasts was visible in the tight light blue zippered hoodie. Her blue jeans were soaking wet on top at her thighs, the rest of her legs not visible, tucked inside the kayak. Charlene knew they were all thinking it was better that she had on clothes.

The deep, red-black, mostly dry bloodied gash that went all

around her neck stood out in the harshness of the lights. A trail of what looked to Charlene like fishing line was caught in the top zippered part of her hoodie, extra she guessed, not needed to strangle Lori. It was this that Charlene saw when she looked up as she and the professor were trying to move the kayak earlier. She knew death had already set in and there was no saving the poor woman.

"I'm guessing it's not suicide then," Joe said.

Officer Edwards helped Joe untie her hands from the paddle. He handed the blue rope to Sarah who put it into an evidence bag. They untied her hands. Sarah put that rope into a separate evidence bag. They put bags over her hands tied at the wrists. Sarah took pictures at every step. Just as Joe and James firmly, but almost tenderly, moved the woman's body down, bending her knees so her head could be seen, exposing the dark blue, unseeing eyes and long tendril of red-orange hair from the side of the hood that was up over Lori's head, Ashley walked up to them and said, "What's going on? Oh my God!"

CHAPTER 33

Charlene

Charlene wasn't sure if she was more surprised at seeing Ashley in front of her or that it was not her in the kayak. She was certain it was Ashley she looked at from under the kayak when it was still on the rack. She had seen the same light blue hoodie on Ashley the past few days. She was thinking about Haiden and the annoying looks Ashley gave him while on the pontoon boat going to the parking lot at the start and end of the students' time out in the field. She had him placed as her number one suspect and she was sure the professor thought it was Ashley as well. Lori had been under the radar since the students arrived, it seemed, so Charlene was shocked to find Lori dead and Ashley alive.

Ashley's cries brought Dan and the three guys out of cottage #1.

"You killed her!" Ashley yelled as she stepped toward Greg.

Officer Edwards moved as if to stop Ashley if she hit Greg as it looked like she might.

"What?" the professor demanded of Ashley.

Greg stood still. He looked from Ashley to Dan to the men and woman in white suits, to the kayak, to the lights, and back at Peter who was right behind him. He looked at the kayak again and made a rush to it but was stopped by Officer Edwards. He had seen the bloated face and thick gash at the neck and his face crumbled as he realized it was Lori in the kayak.

"Where have you been Ash?" Haiden asked.

His question seemed so far removed from the context of Lori being found dead in her kayak, that all Charlene could do was stare at him and try to figure out what the hell he was on about. It seemed that he wasn't the least bit concerned about Lori. It gave Greg some wiggle room, Charlene thought. He seemed to have seized the chance to compose himself as Ashley focused on Haiden and not him.

"I was out in the trails in the back bush. I took my study stuff and sat up there. I got turned around and finally followed the hydro line out. I can't believe no one came looking for me!" she shrieked at them all.

Charlene couldn't believe the way things were unfolding. What a selfish self centred little girl, she thought. Then she remembered that people handle difficult situations differently and she cut her some slack, not much, but a little.

"Professor Bowen told us not to worry about you," Peter offered.

"Professor Bowen had better worry about me!" Ashley yelled as she looked right at the professor.

"Okay everyone. I'm Detective Davidson of the O.P.P. and I want you all to go back inside the cottage. This is Officer Edwards. Either I will come and talk to you soon, or Officer Edwards will." Sarah pulled her face mask back up and gestured with her arms to try to herd everyone back to the porch steps.

"Where are you going?" Sarah called to Ashley who was walking away from cottage #1.

"If you think I'm going inside that cottage with that murderer you are crazy!" Ashley yelled as she started up the steps of cottage #2. "I'm sitting right here so you can keep an eye on me. I might be next!"

CHAPTER 34

Thursday September 24th, 2015

Charlene

She heard her cell phone bleep its alarm. Charlene opened her eyes and thought about coffee. She forgot to get the percolator ready last night so she would have to do it blurry eyed. Thanks goodness she set the alarm last night or she would have slept in later than she should. She slipped on her moccasins and padded out to the kitchen. Her legs were tired and she felt old. It was a long night and standing in the damp really chilled her. Even the hot shower she had before she crawled into bed didn't stop the cramping in her calves in the middle of the night.

She got the coffee from the can in the fridge and filled up the percolator with enough water to make a full pot. Six cups of water would give her three big mugs. Just as she put the coffee on the burner and started to walk to the bathroom to wash up, she almost jumped out of her skin when she heard, "You better have put enough java in that old pot of yours for me too Staff!"

"Oh my God! You scared me Sarah!" she finally managed to blurt out.

Charlene walked back to the kitchen and looked over the table to see the sleepy-eyed detective peak over the back of the chesterfield in the adjoining living room, holding on with one hand as she tried to pull herself upright and push the hair out of her eyes with the other hand at the same time.

"I forgot you were here," she added.

"Well I won't be forgetting I was here this morning," Sarah said giving Charlene an exaggerated eyebrow wiggle.

"Oh shit," Charlene said looking down at herself before turning and taking her naked self to the bathroom.

"Hey. Come back!"

"I'm telling Patty," Charlene replied before closing the bathroom door.

As she washed her face, the events of the night before came flooding back. Poor Lori. Who killed her? Why would he kill her? It would take strength to hold onto that fishing wire that tight, tight enough to cut so deep into her throat and also be able to withstand Lori's struggles. She was sure Lori did struggle. Her face was set into a fierce grimace and her finger ends were all bloodied, probably from getting caught in the fishing line as she tried to get a hold of it and pull it away from her neck. Her neck was all scratched too. What was that all about with Ashley accusing Greg? What was that all about when Ashley yelled at Dan? Greg fell apart as they group walked back to the cottage. What was going on inside that cottage right now? How are Lori's parents taking it? They're not, she thought. They can't even have taken it in yet.

105

Charlene got dressed and went into the kitchen to turn the percolator down to medium heat. Sarah was hopping around and as soon as she saw Charlene she rushed past her and went into the bathroom.

"Christ Staff. It took you a long time," she yelled through the closed door.

"You could have used the office bathroom".

"Now you tell me. Wait. You have an office bathroom?"

For the second time that morning Charlene jumped.

"Sorry Ms. Parker," Officer Edwards said as he walked into the kitchen from the back hall. "You should have locked that door last night like we told you to."

"If I did you wouldn't have been able to just walk in," Charlene said with a trace of annoyance. She saw the look on James' face and apologized. "Sorry James. I forgot I told you to use the key and come in."

Charlene gave him an extra key last night as he was leaving to go home to get some sleep. She knew he would be back early to relieve Officer Wendy Miller who was on crime scene watch all night shift and she didn't want to have to get up to let him in in case she was not dressed, which, she realized, she almost wasn't.

"Is that coffee I smell?" he asked.

"It is but the first mug is mine. I forgot all about Sarah crashing on the chesterfield last night and that you would be back, so I didn't make enough. I'll put another pot on once we all have our first sips. Make yourself at home. I have to get ready to take the students to the landing and be ready for the Porters in case they need something," Charlene said.

"Forget about the students going out today Ms. Parker, at least not so early. After the doc went with the body, I mean Lori, with the body removal guys, Sarah and I took the initial statements from everyone and it took forever, so they were up late. That is everyone but Ashley. Wendy was watching the scene from the front porch of cottage #2 and she told me that Ashley insisted on sitting up with her. She only lasted for a few hours then went to her bedroom though. Rookie. She hasn't come out yet so she hasn't had a chance to talk to anyone. I know that when Tracy and I stayed here for a night last summer that cell phones don't work from inside the cottage so she couldn't talk to anyone by phone either.

"Anyway, Sarah wants everyone at the station for proper video interviews, so they can't do their rock stuff. As soon as Sarah says so, I will relieve Wendy at the scene until we are finished with it."

"When will that be?" Charlene asked, fully expecting not to be able to use that area for a few days or more.

"We won't be much longer Staff," Sarah said coming into the kitchen with a towel around her head. "I hope you don't mind I took a shower."

"No I don't mind. I had a good hot long shower before bed to try to clear my head. If you want another shirt, you're welcome to one of mine."

"Thanks Staff, but I've got a clean suit at the station. I'm going to get James to boat us all over to the landing soon and meet them at the station for interviews. I've got the day shift officer in to monitor the video equipment while I talk to them separately. I have to talk to the Porters first though. James got their info last night but I really wanted to deal with the students and professor first. What was with that other chick?" Sarah asked Charlene.

"That's Ashley. Of course you heard her name mentioned last night. I thought for sure it was her in the kayak. I'm sure that's her blue hoodie Lori had on. There was something going on with her and the other student, Haiden. I'm pretty sure he had a thing for her that she didn't have for him. She was almost cruel to him at times when I saw them together on the boat rides across. Did you catch her yell at the professor too?"

"Yeah I think I better wake her up and get her statement before I walk over to see the Porters. Cottage #5 for them?" Sarah asked.

"Yup. They are early risers and probably want to take the rental boat out soon, so they'll be anxious that you are not there yet."

"I Roger that Staff, the Porters are first then," Sarah said with a mock salute to Charlene. "By the way, thanks for the bowl of stew and buns last night. I didn't think I could eat but I gorged myself so I am still full."

Charlene was happy to have been able to help by feeding them. She put the stew in the crock pot on the table in the office and plugged it in to keep it hot. She set the buns and butter with the dishes and cutlery and told everyone to help themselves.

Sarah and James and Wendy had some but Joe left with Lori as soon as the funeral home guys came to take her on the gurney to the morgue for further examination by Joe today.

Charlene took them over on the pontoon boat, making it easier for them, with Lori's body and the kayak on board.

Even at that late hour the young guys, one of them the son of the funeral home owner, came dressed in dark suits with ties under their wind breakers. The rubber boots didn't detract from the solemn and respectful way they went about their jobs. They too saw things most people didn't, and they would have to deal with seeing Lori like that last night, maybe thinking of their wives or girlfriends or sisters.

"If you want I can take everyone over on the pontoon boat when you are ready," Charlene offered. She wanted to have a look at them all and see what was going on.

"That would be great, thanks. Right now I better get a move on. James, take our boat over to that cottage across the lake and see if anyone is there before you relieve Wendy." Sarah sent Officer Edwards a look that sent him almost running to the door.

"Okay Mum," he replied.

"You've been watching those British cop shows again James. Cut it out."

"Yes Mum," he said as he left.

"What cottage?" Charlene asked.

"The one right across from you. The guys told us last night that some old guy from over there picked them up at the landing yesterday and brought them over here," Sarah explained.

"I thought Dan got them and brought them over," Charlene said. "I keep forgetting there is anyone over there. It sold last summer. I see the boat come and go sometimes but I wouldn't recognize the new owner if I was face to face with him."

"What kind of boat does he have?' Sarah asked.

"A fishing boat and a kayak."

"A kayak? What colour?"

"Yellow," Charlene said.

"Does everyone have yellow kayaks around here? By the way are you sure the kayak Lori was in was your yellow kayak Staff?" Sarah asked.

Charlene took it for granted it was her kayak. It was on her rack. It looked like her kayak. Shit. She should know better than to assume.

"I don't know Sarah," she said. "It sure looked like my paddle. It must have been mine. I paid almost $200.00 for it. It's graphite and strong but really light, and has some scrapes along the side. If it it isn't my kayak and paddle, then I'd like to know where mine are."

"Shit. This is getting worse and worse," Sarah said.

"By the way, Staff, I need a statement from you too. I hate to say it, but I do. It's your place, probably your kayak, and I know how you feel if anyone uses your kayak. If looks could kill, a lot of people would be dead now, just getting close to that kayak of yours."

Sarah smiled. "I'm serious though, I need a statement."

"I knew you would. How about it I type one out on the computer and you can question me later?"

"How about we do that over more stew and buns?" Sarah asked as she turned and walked out of the kitchen and back into the bathroom to dry her hair.

CHAPTER 35

Charlene

Edna and Jack came into the office. Charlene was sitting at the desk staring at her lap top, trying to figure out what to do with guests who were supposed to arrive and go in cottage #4 for the week-end. They were expected to come tomorrow about 3:00 o'clock and leave either Sunday or Monday. They were hoping to watch the eclipse and do some hiking. They only paid a deposit for Friday and Saturday night but hoped to stay Sunday if their sitter could stay over that night too. The young couple lived in Little Current and the woman's grandmother offered to babysit so they could get away for a few days. They had two boys under three-years-old and needed a break. They rented the little cottage close to the lake last year in late September, probably liking the discount for that time of year. Charlene thought she would let them use a canoe for free. Last year they hemmed and hawed asking about the price for renting a canoe and Charlene liked them so she only charged them for one day and not two. They practically hugged her.

That was one of the great things about running the resort. She loved to see guests who truly loved the outdoors, and she knew what it was like to try to stretch a dollar. She did it all the time. The furniture in the cottages was mostly second-hand and mostly more than 30 years old at least, except the mattresses and fridges. All those she replaced with brand new ones the first year before she opened. She hated staying at rental places with lumpy beds or noisy fridges. Anything worth a coat of paint got one, and the old chairs and tables she found at used furniture spots like the Salvation Army or St. Vincent de Paul found a good home in the cottages in a kitschy sort of way that guests seemed to like.

Charlene should have asked Sarah if she could have guests come with the crime scene still taped up, with proper police tape, she noticed this morning. She would have to ask her before she left. She was now in cottage #2 getting a statement from Ashley before heading to the station for the interviews. She guessed Ashley would have to go to the station too for a more formal video interview. She would hate to have to cancel the guests.

"Charlene?" asked Edna

"Hmm? Oh sorry. I saw you come in and then got deep in thought and forgot about you," Charlene said. She knew the Porters were the type that she could be upfront with.

"We figured," Edna said. "You must be in such a state. A murder on your property! That poor young girl."

"Did you meet Lori?" Charlene asked.

"No. We haven't been around to talk to any of the students. By the time we get back and get cleaned up and have a late dinner we tend to stay in and go to bed. We get pooped from all the fresh air being out in the boat and hiking on the little islands we stop at. That detective wants us to pop into the station to give a more detailed statement. We thought we would go from there to the trading post and get some fudge."

"Or ice cream," Jack said. "I love those waffle cones and the ice cream there is so good."

"Anyway," Edna said rolling her eyes in Jack's direction clearly not liking the ice cream idea. "Do you want us to bring you back some fudge?"

"I would love some, but I eat way too much once I start. Thanks for the offer though. I think I will wait until the resort is closed then treat myself then. Do you want me to boat you over?"

"Oh no. We will take the fishing boat ourselves. We're not sure when we will be back and we don't want to disturb you," Edna said.

As Edna turned to leave the office, Jack looked back over his shoulder and gave Charlene a wink before following his wife as he was used to doing.

Charlene closed her lap top and thought she better to some laundry. She had her own sheets to wash. It was another nice sunny day with a stiff breeze, so the sheets would dry quickly on the line. She almost always hung the clothes on the big line that went across the back behind the house. Only the rain stopped her. She provided sheets for the guests and made sure to hang those up to since they loved the fresh air smell. Some guests had never smelled sheets fresh off a clothesline. That she could hardly believe. When a string of sheets were billowing on the line most of the kids did not even know to run through them. She showed one little girl how to time it to run through the sheet when it was carried up by the wind. When the mother saw her running through the sheets she ran out of the cottage and quickly told her to stop and apologized to Charlene. She seemed quite unsure as to what to say or how to react when Charlene told her it was fine, that it was wonderful to see. She too was clearly unfamiliar with the game.

"Charlie. I almost forgot. Edna and I found these glasses when we stopped for a quick late shore lunch yesterday. They look pretty new so we thought we could give them to you. Maybe one of the canoeists or your guest or someone out for a shore lunch will come in here looking for them," Jack said as he came back into the office up to the counter and gave Charlene the glasses.

They did look like new glasses, very funky, like a lot of people in Quebec would wear. She noticed on every trip to Quebec City or at stops in Quebec, that people wore the coolest eyeglasses. Charlene took them and put them on the counter.

"Okay Jack. I will leave them on the counter with a note in case someone recognizes them," said Charlene.

"Thanks Charlie. See you. I'll sneak you a piece of fudge anyway," he said as he left the office.

CHAPTER 36

Bob

Bob rubbed his eyes as he waited for the coffee to drip into the pot. What a late night. He managed to get into bed. It got too dark and he couldn't see anything across the lake so he had one drink, then another, and took his third whisky into the bedroom and sat in bed thinking of what he was going to do next. Then it was morning and he walked out to the kitchen and heard a boat and saw the police boat going across to the landing. They're still at it then, he thought.

He reached for the sugar and powdered creamer in the cupboard and almost banged his head into the cupboard door when the knock behind him at the front patio door made him jump. Shit, he thought, when he saw the police officer standing on his deck.

He went to the door and slid it open.

"Good morning sir. Sorry to bother you. I'm Officer

Edwards. I'd like to talk to you for a few minutes if you have time."

"What's going on?" he asked.

"Do you mind if I come in?" James asked.

"Ah..ah...I was just getting coffee, but it can wait," Bob said as he stepped toward James causing him to step back, and walked onto the deck and closed the patio door behind him.

"Okay," said James, wondering why the guy practically pushed him away from the living room door. Most people around here invite him in and ask if he wants a coffee or a drink or something. He tried to get a look at the inside of the cottage but could only see his own reflection in the glass of the patio door.

"I understand you went over to the resort parking lot yesterday and picked up some guys, the students staying at the resort. Is that correct?" James asked.

"Yeah, I did."

"What time was that?" asked James.

"About three or so. Maybe a bit later. I'm not sure."

"Why did you pick them up?"

"I saw them getting out of the van and figured since I was already out in the boat I might as well give them a lift. There were only three of them and they could all fit in my boat. It would save Charlie, I mean Charlene, the trip," he said.

"That was nice of you, helping out Ms. Parker like that."

"Yeah well she's always so busy so I figured it would save her the trouble."

"Do you know Ms. Parker very well?"

"I've never met her," he said.

"Oh," said James wondering how he knew how busy she was.

"What were you doing on the lake yesterday? I mean, why were you out on your boat and what time were you out?" he asked.

"I go out almost every day in the boat. A bit of fishing and a bit of just being on the lake. I'm not sure what time I went out. I'm retired. Time means nothing to me anymore."

"Where on the lake were you yesterday?" James asked, trying to figure out what questions to ask.

He could feel the trickles of sweat going down between his shoulder blades. It was a warm day and his undershirt didn't seem to be keeping him dry under his uniform shirt and bullet-proof vest over top. He wished Sarah was here to ask the questions. No. He wished Ms. Parker was here. She made him feel like he was making the right choices. He needed some help. He found looking at the guy a bit disconcerting. He couldn't put his finger on why he felt that way, the guy looked perfectly ordinary, at least ordinary for a lot of people he had dealings with. He looked like a drinker, smelled like a drinker, and had a gut like a drinker, but there was something else. Maybe it was his eyes. They were small and dark. He was clean shaven but probably should have had a mustache or something. James noticed his upper lip was a lot smaller than the lower lip. His hair was still in the bed-head position, whatever hair was left was gray and thin and messy.

"I was around the bend up that way." He pointed and James saw that he meant the bay away from the cottage toward the wider section of the lake.

"Then you went the other way some time," James said.

"What do you mean?" he asked.

"Well you pointed that way but the resort parking lot is the other way."

"Oh yeah. I went that way later," Bob said, looking out over the deck and not at James.

"Can you show me your boat?"

"Why?"

"I'm just checking all the boats on the lake, so if you don't mind..."

"Okay whatever," Bob said as he turned and walked down the deck steps toward the dock.

James followed him, careful not to walk right into him on the path. The guy had a limp and moved pretty slow. He noticed the fishing boat had seen better days.

"Well that's an old one isn't it?" James asked.

He noticed the guy was looking at the police boat tied up at his dock.

"Not that one, your boat," he said.

"Oh. Yeah. It came with the place."

"How does the motor run?"

"Pretty good for an old one. It needs to be warmed up before it gets going. It coughs a bit at first...like me," he said, coughing a dry smoker's chest cough in James' direction.

"Johnson's are pretty good, aren't they?" James said, trying to get the guy to talk a bit.

"I guess. It's the first boat I've owned so I don't know," he said. "What's with all the questions anyway?"

"You've got a nice view from here too. I noticed you have

a good lake view from the deck. Did you see a young woman on the shore across the lake or in a boat or kayak yesterday while you were out in your boat or when you were out on your deck?"

"Why?"

"We're investigating a murder. A young woman staying at the resort was found dead yesterday afternoon at the resort. She has, had, long red hair," James corrected himself.

Was he supposed to tell the guy all that? He felt way out of his depth talking to this guy. He practised asking questions with Tracy. She usually just laughed at his interrogations but it was helpful to him to do it out loud. He had some basic training but hadn't been on any in depth interview courses yet. Sarah said she'd recommend that he go to the next one coming up at Police College. Now though, he was practically winging it and he felt sick that he was messing up. Ms. Parker told him once to talk as if he was just having a conversation. He took a deep breath hoping the guy didn't notice, and plodded on.

"We are canvassing all the neighbours and cottagers on the lake to see if they saw the young woman out on the lake or anywhere in the area really, yesterday after about 1:00 o'clock yesterday afternoon. So I was wondering if you saw her."

"How old was she?" Bob asked the officer.

"She was in her early 20s," James answered still unsure if that was appropriate to information to pass on.

"If she was staying at the resort was she one of the students? I know there are two girls in the group." He stopped and as if he sensed what James was thinking then carried on, "Everyone around here knows the students are at the resort. I see them going across the lake on the pontoon boat to their van and sometimes see them climbing up the rock face along the highway."

"Yes she was a student," James said.

"I was never close enough to tell what they looked like, but one girl had long hair, but I thought it was dark brown. I don't know what colour hair the other girl had."

James remembered the hat found in Lori's bedroom in the cottage. He thought he better keep that information to himself. Then he wondered how this guy knew the colour of Ashley's hair if he didn't get close enough. He looked back over the lake toward the resort and thought he would never be able to tell what colour hair anyone had from this distance. Maybe he noticed the hair colour when he saw the group along the highway or something.

"If that's all officer, I'll get back to my coffee. I'm sorry to hear about the death of the girl," he said.

"Okay thanks. If you remember something about seeing anybody with her or anything like that, here's my card, you can give me a call and leave a message if I'm not there."

James passed Bob his card.

"Yeah okay, but I doubt it," he said as he turned to go back up the path to the cottage.

Officer Edwards turned to get into the police boat. As he untied the line he noticed bits of blue strands caught in the rough boards of the dock. He bent down to pick a few pieces up and put them in his pocket.

CHAPTER 37

Charlene

Charlene got the sheets from the linen closet in the storage room and put them in the laundry basket on the long work table. Sarah told her it would be okay to have the guests come to cottage #4 tomorrow. She said the area in front of cottage #1 and the canoe rack would be still taped off so no one could be there though. Charlene wondered how she was going to get a canoe for the young couple to use for their week-end. Then she remembered the Porters brought their canoe with them and thought she would ask them if she could rent it from them. That would be a first. A resort owner renting a canoe from a guest. Now though, it would be good to get the cottage ready.

Charlene added clean pillow cases, toilet paper, a dish cloth and tea towel, a shower mat, a small wrapped soap for the bathroom, and a stack of coffee filters to the basket. She grabbed a set of freshly filled salt and pepper shakers, a package of coffee, an old creamer and one of the small baskets from the storage shelf. She had already cleaned the cottage after the last guests, but wasn't sure if more guests would be using the cottage before she closed the resort, so she didn't stock up the cottage after she cleaned. This time of year she didn't like the sheets sitting on the beds anyway in case the cooler nights got them damp feeling.

Charlene used to make the beds for the guests for the first season then smartened up and put the folded linen on top of a folded blanket at the end of the beds that she made up with the new bedspreads she bought for all the cottages. It was just too much work and most cottages resorts she had stayed at before she bought Kirk Lake Camp didn't even provide the sheets. She knew that these days a lot of tourists preferred to stay just a few nights and didn't want to have to pack sheets. Besides, a lot of her guests flew into Canada from other countries. It just wasn't practicable to pack linen in luggage.

She walked to the small cottage set close to the lake and stopped mid-way savouring the smell coming from the pine needles that were all over the ground. The sun heated the needles up and the scent was heavenly to her. She was careful to step over the exposed roots of the trees on the ground. She noticed she would have to repair a small tear in the screen in the door to the porch. Not a week went by when she didn't have to fix a screen. This time it looked like a fishing rod tip might have poked through the screen. She didn't notice it when she cleaned the cottage last time, but that didn't surprise her. The little tears were hard to see sometimes. She went into the porch and opened the door leading into the tiny living room of the cottage. She loved the smell inside the cottage too. Each cottage had a different smell even though she cleaned them all the same. It was the kind of wood cupboards or furniture or type of trees just outside the cottages that made each one unique.

Charlene put the sheets on the end of the beds. Though she was pretty sure the couple would sleep in one bed, they were paying for two bedrooms so they got two sets of linens. She set the basket on the middle of the table and put the salt and pepper shakers inside with the one complimentary coffee package beside them. She set the antique creamer in the basket. She would go out tomorrow and pick some wild flowers to put in the vase just before the guests arrived. She put the coffee filters upside down on top of the drip coffee maker on the counter beside the sink. She hoped the guests read the note she had laminated and affixed to the cupboard that told them to use the filters and throw the coffee grinds out instead of putting them down the drain. The septic system would last longer if they followed her request. A lot of city people just didn't know enough about living in the woods and septic systems were beyond their interest. Charlene had to be interested though. Plumbers were expensive and she had to call the local company a few times. She smiled as she thought of the apprentices having to go down into the holding tank to fix the pump. It seemed they were all slim and she wondered if this was by design so the older, more experienced plumbers didn't have to go into the septic mess.

The dish cloth was set folded near the tap and Charlene hung the tea towel on the small rod fixed to the wall just below the cupboard. They matched the dark green colour scheme of the little kitchen. Charlene was pleased with the green and white checked table cloth she made for the table. She had a collection of antique creamers that came with the resort. Some were part of a set with a sugar bowl but most were not. She liked filling them with flowers for an old-fashioned added touch that most guests said they appreciated. This one was white with a bright yellow flower painted on the side. If the guests were not allergic to Goldenrod, the tops of the weed would look good in the creamer she thought.

She put the soap at the side of the sink in the bathroom. She opened the shower curtain and checked the shower for any new spider webs. Seeing none, Charlene closed them and hung the shower mat over the top of the shower. That too matched the colour scheme. Some curtains had prints with bears, some with fish and this one had a print of wildflowers against the dark green fabric. She put the extra toilet paper on the shelf below the sink. She only provided one roll usually, but if someone was staying for just a few days she put enough in the cottage for the stay. Guests who stayed for the week had to bring their own toilet paper and food. Charlene shuddered at the idea of running a cottage resort with a restaurant. It was hard work enough having self-catered cottages never mind having to cook as well.

As she was checking the cottage to see if she missed anything, she thought about the quiet boat ride over to the parking lot earlier. Greg and Peter stood their usual sturdy-leg pose, but had their backs to the rest of the group. Haiden sat beside Ashley as usual, but Ashley didn't even try to hide what seemed to Charlene to be disgust at his puppy adoration. The professor didn't sit in his usual chair at the front. He stood beside Charlene as she drove them over. Sarah and Officer Miller were at the front of the boat so that could explain that. It seemed he wanted protection from the situation. Only Wendy and Sarah said thanks and goodbye to Charlene. No one else said a word. Sarah looked over her shoulder when the others were walking to the van and gave Charlene a tired smile.

Charlene took the empty basket back into the storage room and realized she was hungry. She only had one cup of coffee. She never did make the second pot after Officer Edwards left to go across the lake and Sarah left to talk to the Porters and Ashley. She didn't feel like making more coffee now though. She needed food. James was sitting outside at the picnic table in charge of the taped off area. She saw that he had his head down and it looked like he had his cell phone in his hand, probably texting Tracy. It was hit and miss to make phone calls from anywhere on the property, but cell coverage for texting was good enough outside most of the time. She noticed a tarp had been draped over the top of the canoe rack as well as the sides, covering the rack completely. She didn't disturb him, but went up to the kitchen to make some lunch.

There was some stew left, but Sarah probably would be back and probably would want to eat the rest. She didn't cook at all and thought all meals should come from the freezer section and heated up in a microwave. Patty was the cook in that household, but these were her days to be on the road. Charlene took an apple, a sweet potato, an onion, and the remains of a red pepper from the fridge. She cut them all up and put the chunks into a big pot and added some water. She added lots of fresh ground black pepper and a pinch of cayenne pepper powder. She turned on the stove and put the lid on. She would cook up the vegetables then mash them and add a bit of milk and butter. James would likely want some of the soup when it was ready. She looked in the fridge and saw she had a little bit of plain yogurt left. That would be good as a dollop on top of the soup to cut through the hot pepper taste.

She moved around the kitchen and living room tidying up after the police officers. The bathroom was spotless so Sarah obviously cleaned up after herself. It was nice to have Sarah stay over. Who knew what the killer's intentions were. Was Lori targeted? Was it chance and opportunity and it could have been anyone stuffed into her kayak? It could have been her. She didn't really think so though. She thought that because she was older the killer may not have been interested in her. That's just stupid, she thought. That's not the way murder works and she should know better. She did know better.

When Sarah came over earlier to the office to say she was ready for Charlene to take them all over to the parking lot, Charlene asked about Mr. and Mrs. Peterson and how they were taking the death of their only child. Sarah told her police in Sudbury helped them out by going to the Peterson's house and breaking the awful news. The parents were on their way to the morgue at the Espanola hospital to officially identify their daughter. That would be heart-wrenching.

It made Charlene think of her police case when a man was found by hikers at the bottom of the Devil's Punch Bowl, a curved section of the Niagara Escarpment along the top of the mountain in Hamilton. The hikers were not at the bottom, but on the top, the ridge not barred by a barrier. There was a fence near the parking lot but it was an old wood split-rail fence that seemed to merely suggest that people should not go past it.

Charlene and her partner, the senior detective of the team, were dispatched to the scene after the beat patrol officer arrived on scene and knew a body meant CID should be in charge. He was experienced enough to not allow any on-lookers and the area was taped off upon their arrival. It was a warmish spring day, but Charlene had her long suit coat on in anticipation for the cool evening to come. She and her partner walked to the rim of the escarpment and looked down. The vertigo or whatever it was hit her hard. She had to grab her partner's arm and quickly tell him to stop. Charlene felt like a vacuum was sucking her closer to the edge and she felt she would just jump over the edge. The only way to stop the feeling was to step back a few paces and wait until her heart beat returned to normal. She had never experienced that before. She got close enough though to see what looked like a body splayed on a ridge almost at the bottom of the gorge. Her partner took a closer look and he thought it was a body for sure but it was too far down to know whether it was a man or a woman. He led Charlene back away from the ridge, sensitive to her plight, and they walked over to the couple in their twenties who had been out for a walk around the top of the escarpment, obviously not suffering from standing so close to the edge, but suffering because of what they had discovered.

They were leaning against the patrol officer's car. They told them that they also found clothes at the top of ridge. Charlene and her partner left the officer, notebook in hand, to get the details from the couple, and walked to the ridge at the centre of the bowl. Clothes were folded neatly. Socks, underwear, jeans, a button-down long-sleeved shirt, and a light windbreaker. Between the folds of the clothes were lined note paper filled with what appeared to be poetry that included lots of lines about flying and freedom. There were no shoes.

The only way to get to the body was by way of rappelling equipment and that meant the fire department. Six firefighters arrived and they hooked up the lines and safety harnesses around two of them and using pulleys, they descended with a basket large enough for a person to fit inside. It was terrifying to watch, but more terrifying for the firefighters since they had not used the equipment in a real life situation before. No one could be sure if the person was still alive. Though it was technically a rescue operation, they all believed it was a recovery mission.

The faces of the firefighters as they ascended with the body of a man in the basket told it all. He was dead. His naked body was lifted onto a tarp the beat officer got from the trunk of his car in preparation. He used his cruiser, with the plain door car Charlene and her partner drove, to block the body from any onlookers while awaiting the arrival of the coroner. The firefighters and police officers stood quietly in a circle around the body at the centre. His head was severely misshapen, likely from the impact of the fall.

Charlene and her partner had a name and address from the

identification in the pocket of the folded jeans and went to the apartment. The landlord let them in where they found the walls covered in script, poetry and lists of names, and beautifully done sketches of nature with the main them of eagles. Notes were scattered everywhere in the tiny messy apartment. An address book was found and a man's name with same surname and his address were on the inside cover. They drove to the house and the man who answered the door looked similar to the dead man. His wife came to the door and invited them in. They had to tell them the body of a man had been found and they believed he was related to him. It turned out it was the man's younger brother.

They learned the dead man suffered from schizophrenia and had a difficult life from age 20 to 26, the age he breathed his last breath. The older brother said he would drive his own car to the morgue to identify the body. He did not want them to drive him and he did not want his wife to go with him. Charlene remembered how she and her partner were concerned about him because he was showing very little emotion at the news that it was likely his brother in the morgue.

He did identify the body on the gurney as his brother. He said he must have gone off his medications again. He told them that without the help of his pills, his brother often talked of flying. He refused any offer of having someone come to support him or any offer of sitting in the family room off the morgue to collect his thoughts and take some time to digest what he had just seen. He even thanked Charlene and her partner and abruptly turned and started to walk down to the hall to the elevator. He only managed to walk about 15 feet before his legs gave out from under him and he crumpled to the floor.

For some reason, Charlene always thought of this death notification first when thinking about the suffering the family goes through when police arrive at their doorstep with news of a death of a loved one. She had to do many death notifications, some while working uniform patrol. It would almost always be two officers assigned the task. Whether in uniform or in plain clothes, no one wanted to answer the door to police when they hadn't been called, and knocking in the middle of the night was always the worst.

The deceased's car was found parked in the lot at the escarpment and his shoes were side by side, neatly placed on the floor by the driver's seat. Why he took his shoes off to walk across the grass was never figured out. What was figured out was that he stood at the edge of the precipice, opened his arms, jumped, and flew like an eagle.

CHAPTER 38

Charlene

"Hey Sam. How are you doing today?" Charlene asked as she pulled up to the dock to get Sam. "I'm so glad you are back today. It's good to have a familiar face and friend today."

"Why what's up?" Sam asked.

"One of the students, Lori, was murdered yesterday and her body was stuffed into my kayak."

"Whoa. Charlie."

"Exactly."

"You find her?"

"Yup."

"Whoa. Charlie."

They rode the rest of the way over to the resort in silence.

Sam got the paint from the shed and started loading up the basket at the back of the ATV. He liked to drive it behind the house along the edge of the woods and down to the cottage he was painting. He hated the roots that stuck up all along the path from the big pines so he didn't like to walk. Sam was best up high. The ground seemed to swallow him, he once told Charlene.

Seeing Sam made her think of Joe again. She was so tired last night and this morning and so busy she hadn't even thought of Joe. Poor guy would be at the hospital all day doing the autopsy and speaking with Lori's parents. Sam's words came back to her. The boat, the woman, and a yellow kayak. No! Why would Joe be with Lori? He wouldn't be. Charlene's mind started to race and she felt sick, so sick she had to stop and hold her arms across her stomach and hold herself. How would he even know her? He wouldn't. Oh my God, he took fishing line from the office store! Charlene pictured the fishing line pulled tight into Lori's neck. She would have to tell Sarah what she was thinking and what Sam told her. Wouldn't she? Maybe she should talk to Joe first. What should she say? Did you murder Lori? How could she form the words? How could she think he was capable of murder? He wasn't. She was sure of it. Why was she so sick then? Because he was with some woman and lied to her when he canceled their time together that's why. He was on the lake with a woman in his fishing boat towing a yellow kayak. She looked down at her hands. They were shaking. She could barely put the soup in the big mug she took out of the cupboard for Officer Edwards. She got a big spoon from the drawer, put it in the mug, got a plate and put a few slices of buttered bread on it and walked down the stairs. She would take the soup to James first then phone Joe. It was bad enough that he was with another woman in his boat and lied to her, but murder?!

"Thanks Ms. Parker. Are you okay? You look kind of pale. Have you eaten yet?" James asked as he took the lunch from Charlene and placed it on the picnic table.

"I'm okay. I'm just tired and upset."

"Yeah. We're all tired. I'd rather be tired than be in Mr. and Mrs. Peterson's shoes though. Sarah told me Lori was their only child. Nothing's going to be right for them again. Sarah will have to be at the morgue to meet them. I guess she'll head back to the station after they identify the bo..,Lori. Maybe Phil will help us out."

Constable Phil Henderson was the senior officer among the group of officers working out of the station. He qualified to be promoted to the rank of sergeant but had never entered the promotional interview process. He wrote the exams but preferred to work on the street in uniform, even at 43-years-old. As the station's only black officer, he would have a good chance to climb the ranks. Sarah told Charlene she thought he didn't go into the process because he feared he would be promoted and others would think it was because he was black. Sarah and Charlene agreed that many officers would still likely think that even in this day and age. It was the same for every officer in a visible minority group. She and Sarah went into the promotional process anyway, taking advantage of the fact that there were few women officers, never mind any of senior rank. They admitted over a glass of wine or two that they also wanted to stick it to the good ole' boys club that was prevalent in most police departments, or police services as most were called now. They didn't really care that many male officers still felt that women got promoted just because they were women. They knew that for years and years white male officers got promoted because they were white male officers, but they tired of telling them that over and over again.

Charlene and Sarah often talked about how they wanted to get higher in the ranks to be able to make policy changes to help other female officers. When Charlene was an officer, the pants, shirts and police boots were made for men. The hats were too big to fit most women. When bullet-proof vest became mandatory, they were really uncomfortable to wear. They were made for a man's chest. The women though, quickly utilized the space between undershirt and vest as a handy place to put tampons and pads. They never knew when they would be dispatched to something that could take up hours and hours and there was no time to get back to the station or even to the cruiser for supplies. That was when the vest had to be worn under the uniform shirt. It took a few years before the vests had darts to make room for breasts and a few years more before the higher-ups agreed the vest could be worn over the shirt. Before then the officers were told it looked too military or swat-like, so shirts had to come off in order to remove the vest during lunch or dinner. They guys would just take off their shirt and vest and have lunch in their undershirts. It felt like stripping when a female officer did the same thing, so Charlene had to go into the change room each time. The damp white tee shirts in the cool air conditioned lunch room would be cause for an awkwardness best avoided when working so long and so closely together. The hot Hamilton days in July made all the officers drip with sweat under the weight and material of the vests. Charlene always had a supply of fresh undershirts in her locker and would get out of the damp one at a break during the 12 hour shift.

Phil often paid for courses out of his own pocket, courses that were only paid for by the police budget for the select few officers working as detectives. His knowledge of the criminal code and the investigative training he got from the courses were a bonus for the officers at the station. If Sarah wasn't around, Phil was happy to get phone calls even to his home on his days off and make suggestions, always careful to tell the officers that it was his opinion only.

"Ms. Parker? Are you sure you're okay?"

"No it isn't."

"Hmm?" James asked.

He didn't like the way Charlene was acting. She isn't usually so bothered by murder. At least finding the guy hanging last year didn't seem to make her too upset.

"No it isn't ever going to be the same anymore for them. Sorry. My mind is just wandering. If you want more soup just shout. I know you can't leave here even though everyone is gone. I'm going to be in the office. I'll hear you."

"Why don't you get some soup and join me? You'll feel better if you eat. At least that's what my Mom says all the time."

"No. I've got a phone call to make right now. I'll eat after." Charlene saw the concerned look in James' eyes.

"I promise," she lied. She couldn't eat, not yet, thinking of the phone call she had to make to Joe.

Just as Charlene walked into the office and reached for the phone on the desk, the parking lot phone rang. She looked across to the landing and saw Sarah and Ashley at the phone box.

"Hi Sarah. I'll be right over," she said, wondering what was going on.

Sarah gave Charlene the look that told Charlene to keep quiet as she and Ashley stepped off the dock and got on board. It was another silent boat ride back to the resort. After she docked the pontoon boat, Ashley hopped off and started to walk toward cottage #2.

"Wait Ashley. I need to go with you," Sarah said.

Ashley stopped on the path and stood waiting.

"I'll come to the office after," Sarah called back to Charlene.

Charlene watched Sarah move ahead of Ashley and go up the steps into the cottage.

Ashley followed and the screen door slammed making Charlene jump. God she must be tired, she thought. She hated that tired feeling where noises made her body jump as if she didn't expect them. She used to get tired like this after working her sets of night shifts as a police officer. She used ear plugs and a fan in the room to mask outside noises, but she didn't sleep more than a few hours and had to get up and go back to work and do it all again and again and again. The worst was when working in the Criminal Investigative Division where she had to work six 10 hour night shifts in a row. Her body was twitching a few days in, and she used to jump at the slightest noise. Like now.

"Hey Ms. P.," Ashley said as she walked into the office.

"Hi Ashley. Where's Sarah?"

"She's talking to that police officer sitting at the picnic table."

"Where is the rest of the gang?"

"They went for lunch at some Italian place in Espanola that Professor Bowen said burned down but was re-built. They have to go back to the station after lunch. I gave my statement so now I'm going home. I don't think I can stay here with Greg. That detective had to come back with me since the cottage is a crime scene or something and watch me pack."

"That didn't take long."

"I was pretty much packed the same night Greg killed Lori." Ashley said this in such a way that made Charlene think the murder of her classmate by another classmate was an everyday occurrence.

"Why do you think he killed her?"

"He couldn't stand her not wanting to be with him anymore. He's such a loser."

"What do you mean 'anymore'?"

"He and Lori were together for a while," Ashley said as she leaned her arms on the counter across from Charlene in a girl-talk kind of pose.

"They kept it pretty secret so it wouldn't get in the way of class stuff. He got really possessive and she just had enough and called it quits. Besides she hated that he wasn't very smart. He used to bug her all the time for help with projects and essays. She thought it was kind of cute at first then got sick of it."

"Ah. Do the others know Greg and Lori were an item?" Charlene asked.

"Peter is pretty close to Greg it seems, though not like friends. He might know if Greg told him. Lori said she didn't tell anyone. Haiden is too busy thinking about me, so even if

Greg told him, he wouldn't be interested. Professor Bowen probably doesn't know. I can't see Greg telling him."

"Wasn't Greg with Peter and Haiden on the field trip that day though? I took them to the van in the morning and then I saw you and Lori when I was coming back about 1:00 o'clock. The boys all came back together, so how could Greg kill Lori?" Charlene asked, thinking that he could have if the boys weren't all together all the time, or if they dropped Greg off earlier.

But then how could he get across the water? Did Dan pick him up earlier and take him back? Did that guy across the lake pick Greg up twice? Her mind started to race with all the possibilities.

"I don't know Ms. P. but he did it and I'm thinking about going home. It is not a coincidence that the day after they had an argument at the pub she ends up dead. And, he was always bugging her to go in the kayak with him." She stopped and looked at Charlene, then decided to carry on.

"Greg took your kayak out at night when you were in the house. He tried to get Lori to sit on top and straddle it while he paddled. Yeah I know. Gross. She didn't go though, except once in the canoe. They paddled with their hands because the office wasn't open and they didn't want to bug you to get paddles. They just went along the shore and came back. We were sitting by the fire and could hear Greg doing all the talking but we couldn't hear the words. Lori told me later he was really starting to bug her."

"Did she say what the argument was about?" Charlene asked.

138

"No, not really, just more of the same 'baby come back' stuff. And that detective told me Lori was strangled with fishing wire. Greg always went to the end of the dock to fish just before dark. He said he was hoping to catch a bunch of Pickerel for a fish fry. Anyway, can I use the office phone to call home and see if someone will come and get me?"

"Sure but, what about the course. You won't get the credit will you?" Charlene asked.

"I know that's what kills me. Oops! I didn't mean to say that. Poor Lori." Ashley looked at Charlene for a few seconds before she continued, "I know you're probably wondering why I'm not more upset."

Before Charlene could say anything, Ashley said, "I can see it in your face Ms. P. Lori and I had a couple of classes together in the first year and didn't really hit it off. By the time we finished the last three years in a lot of the same class every day, we both realized we didn't like each other. I thought she was stuck up. She would hardly ever come to pub night or go out for a drink. She was always studying. She lived with two other girls in a nice apartment building with an indoor pool and everything. Her parents paid for everything. I had to work at Subway part time all year and then full time in the summer and I was still behind on rent sometimes. I share a place with a guy and a girl, both students from school, and it sure doesn't have an indoor pool. She said she thought I was kind of slutty and was everything she hated about women."

"She told you that?" Charlene asked, marveling at the honesty between the two young women.

139

Taking in the tight tee shirt with the low vee neckline and the plump bit of belly showing above the low hip jeans at the front and the tattoo Charlene noticed the first day at the small of Ashley's ample back, made her realize she agreed a bit with Lori. Not just that but the way she seemed to strut rather than walk.

She empathized with Ashley though. Charlene worked two jobs while going to college and, while she had some help from her parents, she paid for most of her way through three years of college. She hated it when students went off on skiing trips or flew south at the Christmas break and didn't have to work in the summer months but got through college on grant money or money from parents.

"Sure, on the one night she did come out to pub night, when we were planning this field trip with Professor Bowen. Of course that was after I told her she was a snob. She walked off in a huff and Greg and Peter followed to make sure poor Lori was okay. Oh God, there I go again. Sorry. I shouldn't talk like that about her."

"Did Haiden go after her too?" Charlene was trying to keep it all straight to tell Sarah later.

"No. He was in the washroom. It was just me and the professor left at the table." Ashley's head jerked back and her eyes widened.

"Anyway," Ashley said. After a gap of silence and her voice more shaky then it was the night Lori's body was discovered, she continued.

"After that night we agreed to disagree and got along when we had to. We got along pretty well in the cottage considering. We actually had a few laughs, especially about Greg and Haiden. Anyway, I didn't really know her."

Charlene wondered what had upset Ashley.

"Forget about the phone call Ms. P. I don't want to lose the credit. The field trip is almost over and if that detective doesn't let us carry on, the course may be finished anyway, or professor Bowen might just shorten it and pass us all anyway. You know the stress of Lori's murder and being treated like suspects and everything."

Before Charlene could ask her if she told all that to the police, and what made her change her mind about staying, Ashley was out the door.

"Don't go back into the cottage Ashley. Wait with Officer Edwards until I come out," Sarah called back over her shoulder as she opened the door and stepped into the office.

"Hey Staff. She yelled and yelled that she needed to go home and now she isn't."

"She's not for sure?"

"No she just told me she is staying. I don't get her," Sarah said with a smile knowing Charlene would know what she meant.

"The thing is, she can't stay in that cottage so what are you going to do? I told the professor that cottage #2 is a crime scene and he said he wasn't paying for another cottage or even that one for the rest of the stay. Did he tell you that?"

"No. I haven't talked to him. Remember how quiet it was on the boat ride over?" Charlene reminded her. "If Ashley is staying and has to move to another cottage, then the university will have to pay. I'm not covering the cost of her staying in another cottage by herself. Otherwise the O.P.P. can pay, as long as it's not me. I have guests coming into the little two bedroom cottage. Ashley could go into cottage #3. If you have an officer staying on scene then the cottages could be watched to make sure she is safe there, my guests are safe and I am safe here. You better see how deep the department pockets are before I get that cottage ready though."

"Man, you are all business aren't you? You could always have her stay in the house with you. You know safety in numbers and all that."

Sarah took in the roll of Charlene's eyes and hopped onto the counter. She rubbed her eyes and put on the glasses on the counter beside her. "Cool glasses. Hey, I can see!"

"There are chairs over there. Some people sit on them," Charlene said as she shoved Sarah off, holding her hand out for the glasses.

"I didn't know you wore glasses Staff."

"I do. I'm old remember. These aren't mine. Someone left them on one of the islands and Jack Porter brought them in here in case the owner comes looking for them."

"Man am I tired," Sarah said, slumping in a chair.

"The Petersons identified Lori of course. I left them with the doc. I have help with the video interviews. Phil came in and we had two rooms going at once. Officer Miller wandered in too. She said she crashed for a few hours and knew we would need help so she monitored the equipment for us. I know the students are still expected to stay her another week or something, so I can watch the interviews Phil did and if there are more questions I can come back. Phil is better at interviewing then I am anyway. He just has the knack. There's no worry about court issues with the interviews. He's taken about as many courses as me and is qualified.

"Everyone is off having lunch and we'll carry on when I get back. I'm not sure when we'll be finished so I don't know what time you will be called to the landing to get them. The police boat is available but I don't want James leaving the scene. I know it's a lot to expect from you. You can start a bill for the transportation back and forth because it shouldn't be your cost of gas and time. Anyway, I came all this way to drive Ashley here so she could get her gear out of the cottage and get home. I asked her how she was going to get to St. Catherine's but she told me not to worry about it. So I didn't. Now I am. She's going to make the rest of the time miserable for Greg. And yes, before you ask, because I know you are going to, we did interview him first. Wendy was in the van with them on the drive to the station and she told them not to talk about Lori and she said they didn't. Of course they probably talked last night in the cottage even though we got notebook statements at least first"

Seeing the look on Charlene's face, she said "I know, I know, last night was when we should have pulled them in for video interviews but we had the scene to go over. There's just not enough of us to do the job properly sometimes."

Sarah pulled her small frame out of the old rocking chair by the wood stove. Charlene saw that she looked exhausted. Her dark, short hair cut in a pixie style, was sticking up all over and she had dark circles under her eyes. Sarah never wore make-up and looked older and more vulnerable now. Her navy suit pants and jacket were crumpled where the material gathered at her back when she was sitting. Her white long-sleeved shirt still looked crisp though. Charlene guessed it was one she kept in her locker. Sarah normally looked sharp, all angles and energy pulsating around her. Her athletic frame was always moving it seemed. Her dark brown eyes were still sharp though. Charlene noticed Sarah's bare ankles and smiled. She must have ditched the trouser socks she had on last night at the first opportunity today. There were plenty of shifts were Charlene did the same thing after working long overtime hours. She would get up on the counter in the change room and put her feet in the sink and give them a quick wash and soak to revive them before carrying on, including bagging the socks and hoping her boss didn't notice her bare ankles.

"Let's get your statement over with Staff. I'm hungry. Oh, before I forget, Lori's car is getting towed to the station today. The Ident officer from Sudbury had a go at it and we locked it and I have the keys. There was no one to come and tow the car to the compound last night. Our tow guy was called to an accident on highway 17 and was tied up there most of the night and early morning. We didn't know Lori had her car here until Ashley made some comment about how maybe she could borrow Lori's car to get home. Can I leave the keys with you and you get them to the tow guy if I'm not here? Pretty please? Bill that boat ride over too, of course. There's going to be a hefty overtime bill anyway. That's what the bosses get for not having enough of us to do the job properly. They still think nothing happens up here in the north." Sarah walked out of the office toward the stairs leading to second floor of the house.

"Let's get that stew on."

"What about Ashley?" Charlene called to Sarah's back. "What did Greg say?"

"Leave her for now. The little brat can wait."

She ignored Charlene's last question and Charlene would have been disappointed if she hadn't.

CHAPTER 39

Friday September 25th, 2015

Charlene

"Now that's a voice I need to hear right now. I hope you weren't too busy today Charlene and could sit for a bit. I know you have guests and police all over the place. We are finished here for now, so I'm going to get out of my scrubs and go home for a bite to eat and sleep. I hated not taking you in my arms last night. God, what a night for you too. If there's any stew left I'd love to come see you and have dinner with you tomorrow before the special event. That is if the police will let us sit out and enjoy it. Sarah was raving about the stew. She said she would be over to see you later today. Save some for me. I miss you. I love you. Call me back anytime."

Charlene saved the message and listened to it again and again. She sat in the office chair with her morning coffee. Sarah didn't stay over but went back to the station. Officer Miller had come to take Officer Edwards place on sentry duty. Charlene heard her use the key she gave to her. She came in during the night a few times to use the office bathroom and get some homemade banana bread and hot chocolate Charlene left in the office for her. Now though, Charlene had a quiet morning coffee to herself, just as she liked.

Before she realized there was a phone message from Joe Charlene felt refreshed after a good sleep. She was glad she talked to Sarah about him. Now after hearing Joe's voice on the message she wasn't sure what she felt. Bewildered for sure.

The day before had been exhausting. By the time she gave a statement to Sarah about the day when she found Lori up to the time when James arrived on the scene, then told her what Ashley told her, then took Sarah back to her car, picked up the students and the professor, got Ashley settled into cottage #3 on the O.P.P. tab, picked up Officer Miller at the landing, and remembered to get her sheets off the line and make her own bed, Charlene was ready to finish the day by getting out of her work clothes and putting on some comfy yoga clothes. The phone rang from the parking lot though, and the tow guy was waiting for the keys to Lori's car. She made one more run over the lake and signed that she gave the driver the keys. Once back, she put a note on the office door. Though the office was closed for the day, the note told guests she would be doing yoga and would they please just bugger off. That's the note Charlene wanted to tape to the door on some days, but she wrote something more polite that requested guests allow her the time unless there was an emergency.

She uncurled her mat and put the disc into the DVD player set up in the third bedroom. She picked a routine with deep relaxation poses and tried to concentrate on her breathing for a half hour.

After she was finished her exercises, Charlene realized she was famished. She dragged herself into the kitchen. She chopped up some red onion and the last of the stale looking mushrooms and whisked the pieces in with two eggs and a bit of water and fresh pepper. She took some spinach and baby greens from the salad mix in the fridge. Before tearing the large pieces, she poured some olive oil into the bottom of her favourite steel bowl. She added some garlic, a squeeze of mustard, and healthy dash of paprika and fresh ground pepper. She mixed it up and added the torn greens. She splashed a bit of vinegar over top and gave the mixture a toss. Charlene poured the egg mixture into a small frying pan and scrambled it. She ate everything on her plate and looked down wondering where the food had gone. She hadn't eaten all day. She didn't eat any stew with Sarah. She found it made her sick looking at it. The crying jag and conversation with Sarah sapped her strength. She felt like her world was spiraling down.

She had her shower and got into bed. She didn't even bother to go down to remove the sign from the office door. She hoped no one would need her. She needed sleep.

Hearing the phone message this morning brought more tears to her eyes. She didn't doubt that she had come to love Joe. She didn't doubt that he had come to love her. Had that time passed? she wondered. Sarah laughed out loud when Charlene told her what Sam told her about seeing Joe with a woman in his boat yesterday. She laughed until she saw that Charlene was serious. She tried to convince Charlene that Joe would never be with another woman, never mind murder another woman. That led to a long talk, the end result being that Sarah would talk to Sam first before talking to Joe. She told her that much. The tears flowed until Sarah left and Charlene had to pull herself together and get on with the day. Like now. Wendy would want some coffee and Charlene liked to help out if she could. She couldn't investigate anymore, but she could surely get a coffee going for a sleepy-eyed officer who had to sit outside all night.

CHAPTER 40

Charlene

The students and Professor Bowen were allowed to continue their field work. The first day of their planned trip to Sudbury yesterday was spent at the police station giving statements. Today would be a long day with visits to two Inco properties crammed into one. Dan seemed annoyed that the course "had suffered" as he put it to Charlene on the boat ride over to the van. He sat in his usual chair at the front of the boat. Charlene thought he looked more rested and a bit more chipper than she had seen him. One of his students was murdered but he didn't seem too bothered by it for some reason. He complained more that he had to spend a lot of time on his cell phone to the university keeping them updated on what was happening. Charlene gave him a look that he appeared to understand and blushed at his insensitivity. It was a surprise to Charlene that the course was even going forward.

She was more surprised in the change in Ashley. She seemed more subdued and deep in thought, something Charlene hadn't seen in her before. She had been different since she left the office after telling Charlene she changed her mind about going home. Even Haiden seemed to sense the mood shift and was not pestering her as much. Greg and Peter stood beside one another as usual and were both quiet other than a good morning greeting to Charlene from Peter. Greg didn't say anything and did not look at her. Hmm, Charlene wondered what he told police.

Officer Edwards was waiting at the landing as prearranged and hopped onto the pontoon boat as the students hopped off. Charlene took him to his post in front of cottage #2. The back and forth to the landing was wearing on her. Both she and James were quiet on the boat ride and Charlene could see the long shifts were starting to make him look as tired as she felt.

She watched him walk over to the picnic table in front of the cottage and put a small cooler under it in the shade then walk around keeping close to the front of the cottages and canoe rack where he could watch if anyone went near the crime scene. Though it wasn't actually the crime scene as far as anyone could tell, Charlene thought. Poor Lori was dead before she was stuffed in the kayak. There was no trace of blood in the kayak or on the ground. She was killed somewhere else and brought back to the resort. 'Why?' was the big question.

Officer Miller hopped on the boat and sat without much to say. She could barely keep her head from jerking forward as Charlene took her to the landing so she could go home to get some sleep.

She was a pretty woman Charlene realized, taking advantage of Wendy's sleepy state to really look at her. Her hair had come loose from the tight bun she wore to keep her hair tidy and safe when in uniform. The tendrils of soft light brown hair escaped the bun and she didn't look as severe as Charlene first thought. Her light blue eyes reminded her a bit of Joe's eyes. They had the same pale blue milky colour. Her lashes and eyebrows were dark though. Tinted? Charlene wondered. Her skin was a beautiful tan colour not usually seen on people with such blue eyes and fair hair. She was tall and strong-looking, both in body and face, and her Romanesque nose suited the strong vibes that emanated from her. Sarah told her yesterday that Wendy was 28 and had been a police officer with the O.P.P. for six years. She had been stationed in Burlington before being asked to come north just a few months ago. Sarah said she seemed surprised by the north and its lack of services and shopping, being used to the cosmopolitan city ways all her life, but was settling in and was well-liked by her shift mates and the public. She was looking to buy a house in Espanola expecting to stay for a few years at least.

Sam was standing on the dock when Charlene pulled up and hopped on as he usually did without much fanfare. Then he stopped and turned his head and looked at Wendy as she barely acknowledged him and got up from the chair on the pontoon boat and stretched her arms up over her head. She yawned as she stretched then opened her eyes and stared back at Sam. Charlene watched them stand a few feet from one another as they just looked at each other. Well, well, Charlene thought. Then Wendy turned and walked off the boat and down the dock toward her cruiser. Sam stood staring at her as she walked away. "Look back, look back Wendy" Charlene thought, just seconds before Wendy stopped and turned and gave Sam a radiant smile before turning again and getting in the car and driving off.

Sam turned to Charlene and said "Windy eh?"

"Good morning Sam. How are you?" she replied as per their usual greeting.

Once at the resort Sam went into the shed and got organized at what he needed for more painting. Charlene went into the office and picked up the phone to call Joe, then remembered Sarah asked her to hold off talking to him about what Sam said until she had a chance to talk to Sam and Joe herself. She put the phone down and went out to the garden to get a bouquet for the table in cottage #4. The couple would be arriving sooner than the regular check in, and that was okay this time of year. Charlene didn't allow it during the busy summer months when everything had to be cleaned from the departing guests and made ready for the incoming guests. It never seemed it would get done in time.

Charlene had help with the cleaning from mid-June to Labour Day week-end. Linda answered the ad Charlene posted at the reserve down the highway. Charlene paid her well knowing how hard it was to clean quickly and properly. The two of them worked well together and on check-in days concentrated on getting the cottages cleaned. The laundry piled up on the floor by the machines until there was time to do the wash. Charlene had three sets of sheets for all the beds in all six cottages, knowing at times a stain or fray would mean the sheet could not be used again, other than ripped up for cleaning cloths.

After Linda cleaned a cottage and brought the dirty linen in, Charlene went to inspect the cottage, getting on hands and knees and looking under the chesterfield and chair cushions and under the furniture and under the beds. She often found socks and deodorant, crayons etc. when she first hired Linda, but it was rare now to find anything. No one in the area paid as well as Charlene did and she respected Linda for her hard work and Linda respected her in turn. Linda brought Charlene a small bit of moose roast each year as a token of her appreciation. Though non-native she married a fellow from the reserve and they both appreciated the money Linda brought home from the resort. She came in the spring and fall for a week or so and helped Charlene open and close the cottages as well.

Having checked on cottage #4 one more time as she centred the new bouquet on the table, Charlene decided it was time to get the paperwork printed off and ready for the guests. The Porters agreed to having their canoe rented by Charlene for two afternoons only. They wanted to be able to use the canoe in the morning and evening when the winds were down and the lake became calm and serene, the edges of the coloured forest mirrored on the flat surface of the water. Charlene would let the young couple use the canoe at no cost, thinking she would bill the amount of her rental money to the Porters to the O.P.P. since she couldn't get to her own canoe rack.

While in the office, Charlene picked up the glasses Jack gave her and decided she should post an ad in the paper and call the local Moose FM radio station and get a free bit of air time, to let the public know the glasses were found and could be picked up in the office. She took a picture of them with her cell phone, then thought she would just give the make of the glasses and say they were found on one of the islands on the lake and the rightful owner could describe them before she handed them over. They looked really expensive. They were the kind where the frame is hardly noticeable, and the lens were small. The arms were a soft mauve becoming translucent near the tips. The wee bit of frame on top of the lens was clear. They looked like glasses a woman would wear. Charlene packaged them up to keep them safe and put them in the filing cabinet drawer, uncertain what she would do with them if there was no response to the ad.

She looked at the phone and decided she would phone Joe. He did after all leave a message about coming for a stew dinner tonight. There would be no stew and likely no dinner together. Sarah just asked her not to talk to him about what Sam said about Joe being on the lake with a woman in his fishing boat. She didn't say Charlene couldn't talk to Joe at all and she felt she should call him back, even if it would be just to say a dinner together would not happen. She dialed his cell. There was no phone line to his house. Joe's voice message came on. Charlene left a message saying she called and would be out more than in for the rest of the day but would check messages when she could. She hoped the shakiness she heard in her voice did not betray what she was feeling. Knowing Joe, he would worry and she didn't want him phoning her back and acting concerned. That's what it would be, acting. How concerned could he really be. He lied to her and was not in his shop but out on the lake with another woman. Charlene was positive it wasn't Lori he was with. That didn't make any sense to her. It didn't make sense that he would be on the lake with any another woman when he would know that she would likely see them. So what did make sense? Sam must have been mistaken. Charlene was starting to feel foolish for doubting Joe's love for her. Sam wasn't one for speaking out of turn though.

Joe was likely at the hospital. There was the autopsy to do on Lori if he didn't already do it yesterday. Either way he would be busy with the police and reports just as she should be. Come on girl, she thought, you didn't get this far in life by sitting around.

CHAPTER 41

Bob

Bob turned on his laptop and went through the pictures one at
time again. He was getting excited. No one knew he had it in
him. He didn't know he did. What he did know for sure was
that he would keep at it.

CHAPTER 42

Charlene

"Hey Staff. Hold onto those glasses Jack Porter turned in to you. I just found out Lori wore glasses and we didn't find any with her or in cottage #2, or in her car," Sarah said to Charlene over the phone.

"You're too late Sarah. A woman called from the landing about the glasses. The radio station put it out on the air pretty fast after I called. Some young woman thought they might be hers. She drove in about half an hour ago and described them to me so I took them over to her. She said she was on the lake with a friend and they stopped at an island to swim and forgot her glasses there. She said she had no idea where she left them until she heard the radio bit," Charlene explained.

"Shit, shit, shit. I was hoping they would be Lori's."

"You looked everywhere I guess around the canoe rack too, right?"

"Um yeah. Of course we did Staff. What do you take me for? I know I'm not a big city detective like you were, but I did remember to look 'everywhere' by the canoe rack."

"Sorry Sarah. It slipped out. Are you coming over? Late lunch?" Charlene offered as a way of apology.

"No. I'm too busy here at the station going over the interviews we did. By the way we are finished with the kayak and it is yours. Your name is inside the hatch at the back. I'm guessing it's your paddle too since you have the same one and it was in your kayak. Can you come get it from the station? Officer Miller only has a car or I would send it with her when she relieves James. Oh, he has a truck. I can get him to drive his truck to your place next shift out there and throw, I mean, nicely stow it in the back."

Charlene heard the smile in Sarah's voice and knew her apology was accepted. She reminded herself her policing days were over and to butt out.

"Well, I won't be using it much since I'm really busy with guests and Thanksgiving and then close-up. If James could bring it anyway I would still like to try to get out on the water."

"Brr. It's got to be really hot for me to be out on the water. You know me and boats anyway," Sarah said.

Charlene knew full well Sarah did not like to be on a boat. The pontoon boat was tolerable for her since she could just walk on and off the deck. Sarah told her she was afraid of being in a boat and tipping over. When she was a teenager her best friend's Dad took them out in his small boat. When her friend was overzealous in reaching over the side of the boat to feel the water, the fishing boat tipped over to the side quickly and Sarah's friend fell into the water just as quickly while the motor was still going. She got caught up in the propeller and died. Sarah said she still has nightmares about that day.

"Where could Lori's glasses be?" Sarah wondered. "I have a feeling that the glasses could be a key to finding the crime scene."

"I don't think I ever saw Lori with glasses," Charlene said.

"Ashley brought it up in her interview. She told me Lori was wearing glasses the night the students went to the Black Cat pub. I can't remember off-hand how that topic came up, but I think she was just telling me how good Lori looked and how happy she looked at the pub and that she was glad. She said Greg was a dick so she was glad to see Lori sprucing herself up for the pub night, and how she looked different when she wore her hair down and wore her glasses."

"Did she give you a description of Lori's glasses?"

"Yeah. She said they were purple or something."

"The glasses Jack found were purple too. I guess that's a popular colour now," Charlene said.

"I'll see if Ashley or any of the other students have a picture of Lori on their cell from the pub night so I can get a look at her glasses. I'll let you know so you can keep a heads up out there for me if you see them around the resort or someone turns them in."

"Okay Sarah. Hey, have you had a chance to talk to Sam or Joe?"

"Sam yes Joe no. Sam told me pretty much what you told me he told you. I'm not buying it Charlene but I will have to talk to Joe for sure as soon as possible. I left a message on his office voice mail and cell and sent an officer to his house but he wasn't around. Don't give him a heads up."

"What do you take me for? I know I wasn't some provincial-wide hotshot detective, but I do know what I'm doing."

Charlene smiled at the click on the other end of the phone. She had spent enough time on the phone anyway and had work to do. The couple for cottage # 4 would be coming any minute. As she hung up the phone, the landing phone rang, and she went out to the boat to go over to get them.

CHAPTER 43

Dan

Professor Bowen thought there was something different about the way Ashley had been behaving for the last few days. Sure there was the murder of her classmate and cottage-mate, but for some reason that tragedy seemed to have the opposite effect on her. She looked more at peace and was getting along better with everyone, including him. She engaged in discussions at the Inco presentation at one of their biggest mining sites. Vale Canada he guessed he should remember to call the place since the Brazilians took over in 2006 and the mining operations first became known as Vale Inco then now Vale Canada. She even smiled at him ever so slightly, but it was a smile, and his first thought was that her devious little mind was up to something. He wondered if she concocting some exaggerated version of the fire pit situation just for spite. As he looked at her longer, however, her expression didn't seem to fit what he was thinking about her.

The course was still up and running thank God, he thought. If the university cut the field trip it wouldn't take long before his job would be under the microscope and with fewer students enrolling in geology overall, he may find himself out of work with a monthly divorce payment to make. He would have to move from St. Catherines and hand his resume out in the field and at his age the chance of getting a job would be next to nil. The police all over the resort everyday made all of them nervous, him especially. He didn't tell that detective what was going on between him and Ashley. She pushed him hard about his relationship with Lori though. He said little and what he did say was nothing that could get him into trouble. Greg was probably high on their list of suspects out of the whole group. Who knew that he and Lori were having a relationship? How did he miss that? He figured it was because Lori was so quiet in class that he didn't really know much about her personal life nor did he care...until he saw her at the pub. Wow. What a beauty.

CHAPTER 44

Charlene

Charlene got the young couple settled with the payment of the cottage and after explaining that they could use the canoe during the afternoons but had to dock it at the Porter's dock after use and leave everything clean, they grabbed the life jackets and boat emergency kit Charlene gave them and ran out of the office, both beaming at the free use of the canoe. They made it to the Porter's dock and back to the office within minutes looking for paddles. Charlene had forgotten to get them sized up for the paddles in the office. The Porter's had expensive ones and didn't want to lend them out. It always surprised Charlene that people had no idea that paddles had to be a good individual fit. Most people thought any paddle would do. She explained that the handle of the paddle should come to the armpit as a guideline for size, but also told them that some people prefer them a bit shorter or longer depending on comfort when paddling. They tried various sizes and decided they would come back to the office and switch paddles if needed. They raced out to the Porter's dock once again.

Charlene went over the guests and what they were doing.

The professor and the students were still in Sudbury and not expected back until about 7:00 o'clock because of their crammed schedule. The guests in cottage #4 had a canoe in case they wanted back over to their car. The Porters had the rental fishing boat so they could get over to the landing. Sam was painting the trim on cottage #3 since Ashley was gone and couldn't say Sam was peaking in on her while on the ladder painting the window trim.

Charlene remembered along discussion in the office when a woman came in to complain that Sam had been a Peeping Tom. Charlene tried to convince her that he was just painting but the woman would have none of it so she made sure there was no window frame painting while guests were in the cottage. She smiled remembering that the whole time the woman was yelling about the intrusion on her privacy, Charlene was thinking it was more fanciful wishing on her part that Sam be looking at her through the window.

Sam knew to take a canoe if he decided he had enough painting and wanted to head home to his kids if Charlene was out. Charlene would just put it on the pontoon boat and bring it back. He had keys to the office so he could grab a paddle and life jacket if it was locked. James was on police duty stationed over at the canoe rack at the picnic table. He knew he could come in and use the bathroom in the office if he needed to and find Sam if it was locked. There was shade he could get into and it was another gorgeous fall day.

The art show would be on in the village up the highway. Artists gathered at the community centre the last week-end of September each year and set up booths to sell their works of art. That attracted a lot of people into the area to the festival and they put their boats and canoes onto the lake or hiked out in the woods among the quartzite rocks and pine trees to try their own hand at creating what Charlene though could never be replicated. The natural beauty was satisfying enough to her.

She thought back to guests who were part of some church group and rented cottage #1 for a week-end during the fall colour peak a few years ago. They asked about hiking trails and she explained the trail that was really just the deer run through the back forest behind the resort, but since it meandered up the high hills, there were quite spectacular views from the summit along the white and pink quartzite rocks. Charlene told them to follow the trail tape she tied around branches at intervals to keep the guests on her property and gave them a printed map of the trails. The group of six young men and women went off toward the trail excited and chatty and came back into the office a couple hours en mass. They said they must have been lost or the map was wrong or something because they couldn't see any spectacular view. They said all they saw were rocks and trees and the lake below. Charlene remembered that she almost laughed thinking it was a joke, then realized they were serious. They really didn't get it. They didn't see the forest for the trees. She remembered thinking as well that since they were religious they would especially understand the spirituality of nature itself and be able to appreciate its beauty. Man, oh man she thought, as she gazed at the colours of the trees around the shoreline through the office window. She was glad she got it.

She realized she better head over to talk to Officer Edwards to let him know that she was going to be away from the resort for a bit and if he needed to get over to the landing he could just find Sam and he could take him over in the fishing boat Charlene kept at the dock for her own use or a quick rental.

The police boat had been pulled off the lake since Charlene agreed to be the ferry service for the police for a nice fat fee to end the season with extra income. All her other fishing boats, except for the one the Porters were using, were pulled onto shore. Insurance wouldn't cover them if they were just sitting in the water, so she had to pull them in and out after each rental. It was a lot of work to keep seven boats at the ready but it was good rental income and most of the summer all the boats were rented out. Return guests knew to book the boat in advance and pay the 50 per cent deposit on it along with the deposit on the cottage rental when they phoned in their reservation plans.

First though, she needed food and she would share with James too. Peanut butter sandwiches were not enough to get a young man through a 12 hour shift, and knowing him and what he said about Tracy, that was likely all that was in his cooler. She went out back and picked a few sweet yellow tomatoes that were still in the garden at the back of one of the outbuildings facing south. She saw that there was a small hole in the chicken wire she had all around the slats she made into a garden box. The bears, rabbits and deer roamed the resort and she learned the first year that her vegetables were a tasty meal for the animals along with most of her hostas and flowers that she planted in the garden beds around the front of the house and office.

She put her soup pot on the stove and added the tomatoes, a bit of water, garlic, lots of black pepper, and torn up bits of fresh summer savoury and chives she cut from the garden. She added frozen corn, chopped sweet onion and a handful of green lentils. She threw in a blob of butter and turned the stove up while she got changed to go out. Work clothes were good for around the resort, but Charlene liked to put on her "going to town clothes" before heading off the property.

She had noticed the red light on the office phone blinking when she was getting the paddles for the guests. After they left the office, Charlene checked her messages and there was one from Joe. He said he had to leave town suddenly and would call her later. His plan for dinner with Charlene that night was not going to happen.

CHAPTER 45

Bob

Bob closed his laptop, feeling again the rush of excitement when he looked at the pictures. He wished the police would get off the resort property. He noticed the police woman looking over at his deck suddenly a few times. She may have caught him with the binoculars. He had to put them down while she was on duty and he got antsy when he couldn't look over. The male officer was on duty today though, so he risked putting the powerful lens to his eyes. He thought the police must be pretty certain that no one at the resort was the main suspect or why else would they let the students move about so freely and he noticed new guests checked into cottage #4. They wouldn't let the resort operate like normal if they suspected someone there would they? He didn't really know. Other than a date at court for trespassing when he was 16 he kept himself under the police radar all these years. When he was taking a shortcut along the rail line to school he got caught by some rail officer and had to go to court. Bob also did a lot of drinking and driving in his days like a lot of people his age, with one for the road, literally, but managed to make it home without getting stopped. He knew better than to drink and drive now though. He saw Charlene get on the pontoon boat. She looked up quickly as she was untying the lines from the dock. Shit. He put the binoculars down.

CHAPTER 46

Charlene

Charlene turned off Highway 6 to the dirt road into the small village. She felt a bit on edge. What was that flash of light she saw out of the corner of her eye while at the dock? She had seen it before a few times. She made a mental note to call the optometrist when she got home and get her eyes checked. She'd heard about that condition where people see flashes of vertical light when they turned their head quickly. Had the flash of light caused her to turn her head or did she turn her head quickly and that caused the flash? She couldn't remember. She smiled to herself as she thought that at her age she couldn't remember a lot of things. Menopause had its drawbacks and keeping stuff in her head for any length of time seemed to be one of them. She and Patty laughed about the trials of getting older every time they got together. Sarah poked fun at the two of them but they both knew Sarah would get it in another 10 years or sooner when she starting getting hot flushes, night sweats, little sleep and couldn't remember anything if it wasn't written down. Ah, youth, Charlene thought. Though as much as there was tribulation in getting older, she wouldn't wish to repeat the angst that came with youth either.

She got out of her car at the cluster of mail boxes to get her mail. It was only a 10 minute drive from home. Sometimes she walked to get her mail along the old rail line that ran from up behind her parking lot past Miner's Village and along the highway to the small village where there was a convenience store and gas pump. She couldn't do that with guests at the resort though. It took a couple of hours to get there and back when she walked. She walked to the Black Cat pub in the village a few times during off season to have their delicious wings so she could walk them off on the way home.

Charlene could smell food. She realized she was getting hungry. The soup was good but she only had a small mug as she caught up on some office work before leaving. James was working on his second bowl when she left him at the picnic table.

The community centre across from the mail boxes was humming with activity. The banner was up for the art show and there were tables and canopies set up outside as well as inside. Cars were already lined up along the quaint country road and the festival had just started. She saw people setting up speakers under a tent and a few men and women with guitars milling about and arranging chairs in front of what looked like a small stage. Music was a new addition to the art show. Charlene guessed that like most festivals, the organizers had to try different things to draw in the crowd and keep them there. She didn't like the way small art shows or markets became so obviously commercial. Sure hawberry jam from Manitoulin

Island was expected to be marketed locally for the tourists who traveled through Highway 6 from the island to the Trans-Canada highway or the other way to the Chi-Cheemun ferry crossing at South Baymouth across the Georgian Bay waters to Tobermory. The jam and the historical swing bridge at the Little Current end of Manitoulin Island were a few of the tourist must-dos. Hawberry jam was sold at most trading posts in the area, a unique berry found on the island that helped stave off scurvy in the past, supplying the much needed vitamin C to the residents. Charlene learned this after she moved to the resort. She also learned that people born on Manitoulin Island were called Haweaters. She was given a Haweater coin by the young couple in cottage #4 last year as a token of their appreciation as a tip she guessed. The one dollar token coin was minted from 1969 to 2001 and depicted the many festivals and touristy things to do on the island. But she wondered what a booth selling tee shirts made in India with "I'M WITH STUPID" printed on the front and an arrow pointed to the side, had to do with art.

Charlene found the food source and bought a barbeque sausage on a bun from a smiling middle-aged man standing beside a woman wearing a "I'M WITH STUPID" tee shirt. He looked up from the barbeque at Charlene, saw her look to the woman and then to him, shrugged his shoulders and smiled, as if the arrow on her shirt was going to point his way no matter what he did or said.

Charlene loaded the sausage up with ketchup and hot mustard and made her way back to the car. On the way she noticed a booth with information about the rare total eclipse of the moon happening in just a few days. It was going to be a rare event because it was also a harvest moon, the full moon closest to the fall equinox in the northern hemisphere. The dark red-brown colour of the eclipsed moon would be visible from around 9:00 o'clock until just after midnight. She tucked the brochure into her back pocket knowing she would forget all this info by the time she got home and Joe would be interested. What that had to do with art either she didn't know. Sky art? She smiled at the possibilities of such an art medium.

It reminded her that she was hoping to have been with Joe on that night either sitting on a dock or on the pontoon boat floating out on the large part of the lake, blanket over them, hot drink in hand, watching the moon. Where was he? Where out of town did he go? Did Sarah's messages scare him off or did he go before she tried to reach him? Did he even go? She wondered. Would he be back in time for them to see the eclipse together? Her cell phone was vibrating in the car drink holder. She got in to answer it and closed her window against the festival din.

"Hello?"

"Hey Staff. Two things. I got a couple of pictures of Lori wearing glasses. Ashley had one of Greg and Lori sitting together at the pub table and neither of them looked happy. It almost looks like she and Greg just had words. As well, the professor had one and sent it to my phone too. I don't know why he had one of her alone, but it shows Lori perched by the bar wearing her glasses. In the photo he took though, she is looking radiant. I hate seeing the pictures of homicide victims in one way. I'm not sure why," Sarah said.

"Maybe it brings the polar opposites to mind so clearly. It makes it so much more awful to see her dead and then seeing a picture of her so alive."

Charlene felt she knew what emotions Sarah was struggling with. When she was a detective the pictures of victims were hard for her to look at too. She found it easier looking at what death had done to them in reality than looking at the photos families had of their loved ones around the house. She could deal with the death better than the depiction of a life that would never be again.

"Yeah I guess. It makes me sick to my stomach whatever it is."

"Number two?" asked Charlene.

"I got through to Joe on his cell. He's in Hamilton. You're not going to like this. He's at his ex's house."

Charlene felt her stomach clench and felt the tremors start in her knees and travel up her legs. Shaky knees were her body's way of telling her something was not right.

It didn't take much to trigger her memory of driving a police cruiser in the first year as a patrol officer and involved in a high speed car chase along Barton Street in Hamilton. The suspect was wanted for robbery at gas stations using a rifle. Another officer saw a licence plate without a valid sticker and asked dispatch to check on the licence plate as he drove behind the car. Dispatch came back with the information that the owner of the car was a wanted man. The officer thought the driver matched that of the suspect and activated his roof lights and siren, and asked for back-up. Charlene was the officer in the next beat, so was in the area quickly. A car pulled out suddenly in front of the lead officer and Charlene was able to pull out ahead from a side street. She was now the lead car and the adrenaline coursed through her. It was going to be a fight not flight scenario, at least that's how she saw it since she was expected to know what to do, and call out to dispatch what was happening and take control of the chase. Her knees were shaking as she drove, so much so that her foot on the gas pedal was shaky too. At the next red light the suspect stopped. She remembered thinking that it was odd that he stopped. Her knees started to shake even more. She stopped behind and to the left of the car with the cruiser motor acting as a barrier. The second officer pulled his cruiser to the side and back and a third officer pulled out from the side parking lot at an angle. It was just as they practised at police college over and over again. All officers got out of their cruisers and knelt behind the car door, shielding themselves as much as possible. Charlene used her loud speaker and ordered the suspect to turn off the car engine and put both hands out the window to the roof of the car. All three officers had their guns out and pointed at the driver. She ordered him to keep his hands visible and open the car door using the handle on the outside. He complied and was kneeling on the road with legs spread and hands on his head when she approached from behind and told him to lie face down and told him she was going to handcuff him. She put her gun into her holster once he was on the ground with hands behind his back. The other officers had their guns pointed at the suspect, ready to shoot him if he made any move to reach into his pockets for a weapon, or reach for

Charlene or her gun. Once handcuffed, the other officers put their guns away. Charlene searched his pockets and removed his socks and shoes, checking for knives or small blades. They were taught that a proper search before the suspect was put in the cruiser was the safest way to ensure no one would get hurt on route to the station or inside the custody area. Once searched, they pulled him to his feet and put him in Charlene's cruiser. It was only then that she noticed her knees were no longer shaking. The officer who started the chase followed her to central station so they could both take him into custody. It was always supposed to be two officers. Sometimes officers said they would do it alone, but Charlene always asked for another officer when transporting a prisoner to custody. She always planned on getting in her own car at the end of the shift and going home and didn't shortcut on officer safety.

She started to think of another shaky knee experience on night shift when she pulled her cruiser into a dark parking lot in the north end and saw three people in a car. One man got out and walked toward her cruiser and her knees started to shake. It turned out he was wanted for a sexual assault on a young girl while she was in the bathroom alone at school. She shook off the memory.

Jolted back to the present, Charlene had that same visceral feeling and it spread until she started to hear a humming in her ears and her vision went blurry with tears. What the hell was Joe doing? He was with a woman on the lake, possibly Lori, then her murder, and now Joe with his ex-wife? Shit, she was ashamed to feel that hearing about him being with his ex-wife was making her feel worse than the murder of Lori or wondering if Joe murdered Lori. Now she could understand how that poor woman in Hamilton felt when she told her that her husband was burned to a crisp in another woman's garage and that he was up on sexual assault charges against a young girl. She guessed that feelings just came as they came and to explain them was moot.

"Charlene? Did you hear me?"

"I heard you," she managed to say as she smoothed her hands over her knees.

"He's going into the downtown police station in Hamilton and is going to give a video statement to a detective in Major Crimes. He's probably there now. He said he'd head right over. I'll talk to him when he's back as well after I've had a chance to look at the video. They said they'd courier it so I'd have it tomorrow.

"Did he say why he was in Hamilton, never mind at his ex's house?" Charlene asked, not certain she was ready to hear Sarah's answer.

"I didn't ask. You know Staff. It's better to not reveal much before the interview and that includes chit chat. Anyway, I stand by what I said. I don't buy it that Joe would be with another woman, as in having an affair or one-off, or be capable of murder. Besides no one, including you, saw anyone launch a boat at your landing that day. That's the only way onto the lake except for canoes or kayaks from the few steep backyards in Miner's Village. You can't get a fishing boat down those slopes easily without a lot of rigmarole and without anyone noticing. We canvassed the whole village and anyone up at their cottage the days up to Lori's murder. No one saw a boat launch at your dock, or down the steep slopes of the yards that back onto the lake. So...if it was Joe how did he get his boat on the lake? The killer must be someone on the lake already."

"Have you had a look at Joe's boat?"

"No. His place is locked up and we have to wait. We don't have enough to get a search warrant either. You know that. Hey, where are you and why aren't you at the resort. Slagging off?"

"That's number three, four and five. You said two things."

"In other words you're saying it's none of my business. I get it. What happens when you resort people get some freedom and leave the property is anyone's guess. You're probably eating some junk food and sticking your tongue out at tourists. Don't go to Joe's place either Staff! I know you. Staff...Staff..."

Charlene hung up and looked down at the last half of her sausage. She had lost her appetite. She got out of the car and walked over to the bear-proof garbage container next to the mail boxes. She put her hand under the handle, felt the latch give and opened the top and quickly threw the sausage in before any bees that were in the container could get out. That's all she needed was a bee sting to send her to the hospital. There was no way she was going to jab herself with the Epi pens she was supposed to have with her at all times. She'd been caught anyway. What kind of food was that to eat anyway? Comfort food, she thought, and she needed comforting, but from Joe and answers from Joe, not food.

As she pulled up Joe's driveway, Mr. Blake from next door

came running over. He'd been bent over in his large vegetable garden when she pulled up. Cripes he moved fast, she thought. Charlene couldn't remember his first name. Ned? Something like that. Yes Ned, she remembered. Joe always called him Mr. Blake, maybe so the Dr. Suess rhyme in the One Fish Two Fish Red Fish Blue Fish book 'Hello my name is Ned...my head sticks out of bed...' won't stick in his mind all day. That should make Charlene smile, but not today.

"Charlene! I have missed seeing you! I tell Joe to tell me when you are coming so I can show you my garden."

"It's good to see you Mr. Blake. You know it's hard for me to leave the resort property when I have guests."

"Oh good for you! You have guests still coming this late? Oh yes, the fall colour time. Did you happen to see how the art show was doing on your way?"

"Yes the cars were lined up along the road into the village and it looks like another busy show, or festival or whatever it has turned out to be now."

"I think I'll skip checking my mail box until it over then. Anyway, are you here to see Joe? I didn't see his truck early this morning. I was going to use my key later if I didn't see him come back in a few days. If you have guests I'd be happy to check on things so you don't have to worry about leaving the resort."

Charlene put a smile on her face she hoped was convincing and said, "I was just passing by."

She didn't want to tell him Joe hadn't asked her to come, nor did he tell her where he was going and for how long. Mr. Blake would wonder at what was going on between them.

Though in his late 80s, he was spry and as active as any 60-year-old, and as curious as any three-year-old. He lived alone in a modest cedar-sided bungalow facing the waterfront on a two acre parcel of prime waterfront property. Many Americans who traveled to Manitoulin Island for the summer were itching to get their hands on it. They'd likely raze the house and build a super big monster home. Joe would hate that. Now Charlene would have to think of what to say to Joe when Mr. Blake told him she was there. It was a certainty he would tell Joe he spoke to her. Shit. Now how was she going to check to see if Joe's boat was at the dock?

"I was sorry Joe had to cancel you coming a few days ago. I had some beets picked for you. I gave them to Stacy at the store. She's been having a hard time of it since Bill left. I can pick some for you if you have the time to wait," Mr. Blake said with enthusiasm hoping to keep Charlene there for a longer visit.

Stacy and Bill Smith were the owners of the general store in the village. They bought the store for their retirement but just one year after they bought the store and a few months into the refurbishing the interior, Bill left and took all the money from their bank accounts with him. Stacy was running the store herself and though looking more haggard, Charlene noticed that after getting through a couple of months without Bill, she was coming back to her old self again. It was Stacy the customers preferred anyway, so the community rallied around her. Charlene realized it had been a few weeks since she had stopped in to see her. She better go in and see her on the way back.

"I would love some beets, thanks. Yeah I was looking forward to some time with Joe. All my guests were taken care of and I had a bit of time."

"He was working like the dickens to get that motor fixed. I went over to his shop for a chin wag and he told me you were coming for lunch. Too bad the motor didn't co-operate though and he had to cancel you and spend more time on getting the motor running for that lad. The poor guy was so upset he wouldn't be getting his boat on the lake for a go at fishing, he was practically crying. Anyway, it all worked out in the end. Now, I'll go get a basket and let's get you some beets."

Charlene parked the car and walked to the garden.

"So, I guess Joe got the motor fixed then?"

"Hmm? No. He needed to slow down he said and take his time with it. That's why he let the young man borrow his motor. I would have thought you knew this. Have you not talked to Joe?"

"We've both been busy Mr. Blake. Joe's been on the murder case and I've had a murder on my property and police there and guests and..."

"Of course what was I thinking? You've had no time to yourselves never mind with each other!"

"So Joe let the guy have his motor?"

"Yup. Joe told the guy to just take his motor off his boat. The young fella could barely contain his delight. He backed his trailer up near the dock and hauled Joe's motor off the boat and onto his own boat faster than I've ever seen it done! He was a big strong man and it didn't look like he had to strain to dead lift the motor up and onto the dock."

"What time was all this? Did the guy say what lake he was going fishing on?"

"No I have no idea what time exactly, maybe before noon or so since I came up to the house to make lunch. I don't know what lake. I left while Joe was still talking to him. What's this, a quiz show Charlene?" Mr. Blake laughed at his own quip and picked more beets, pulling at the dark green of the tops with one hand and loosening the soil with the other.

"When did he come back for his motor?" Charlene asked, feeling her heart bursting.

"I'm not sure. I was working at the dock crib for the rest of the day so I'm not sure," he said as he looked up into the sky, then shook his head. "I'll have to think about that."

"Anyway," he added, "That's the evening Joe had to go to your place for that poor girl. Joe told me there had been a murder when I saw him later looking dead on his feet. He said he was just home to try to get some sleep. Here you go. Those beets will be tasty for you."

Charlene took the basket but not before giving Mr. Blake a kiss on the cheek and a big hug. She quickly went back to the car feeling better than she had for days.

CHAPTER 47

Charlene

"Okay. Let me get this straight Staff. Joe's neighbour told you Joe lent his motor to a guy who was having motor trouble. This guy had Joe's motor on his boat out fishing on some lake some time the same day that Sam told you Joe was on this lake with a woman in his fishing boat, towing a yellow kayak. Correct?" Sarah asked as she sipped her tea in the office by the wood stove.

"Correct. But, Sam didn't tell me he saw Joe, remember? He said he didn't see the man but said he knew the motor sound was Joe's motor. You know, that awful hiccup sound Joe's motor makes that he hasn't fixed yet."

"There are a lot of lakes in the area for fishing. How do we know this guy came onto this lake? Besides, no one came on the lake that day remember?"

"No one saw anyone come on the lake you mean Sarah. We can't assume that because no one saw a boat launched, that it wasn't launched."

"Yes, yes, I know what assuming does."

"It makes an ass out of you and me," Sarah and Charlene said at the same time.

They laughed and sat in silence drinking their tea. Sarah had come to the resort to get look at the canoe rack area again. She was worried about Lori's glasses and wanted them found. She and Officer Edwards went over every inch in cottage #2 again when she arrived, but other than finding an elastic hair bands under a dresser belonging to Ashley, they found nothing.

"At least you can rule him out Sarah. Joe will know the guy's name since he was fixing his motor."

"Yeah. Don't get your hopes up though Staff. There are a lot of lakes around here for good fishing and a lot of old motors on them. Hey don't roll your eyes at me."

"This is serious Sarah. If it was that guy that Sam saw using Joe's motor, then it clears up a lot of stuff about Joe. Maybe Mr. Blake will remember Joe being in his shop working on the guy's motor the afternoon Lori was murdered."

"If Joe's neighbour can give us the time frame that he saw Joe in his shop or at home for sure. You said he left while the guy was still talking to Joe. We need more information Staff. Maybe he will remember the guy bringing the motor back an hour later and that would still give Joe time to get on the lake."

"I know so please Sarah will you go talk to Mr. Blake?"

"Yes. I will head over from here. It still doesn't clear up how someone could launch a boat on the lake without anyone seeing."

"It would be the same question if it was Joe on the lake," Charlene said.

"That's exactly what I've been saying! It has to be someone already on the lake. I told you I don't buy it that it was Joe who Sam saw. A lot of boats have motors that run rough. If Joe's neighbour vouches for Joe, then we have to concentrate on the cottagers on the lake, or your guests. "

"I can't see the Porters killing Lori. Can you?" Charlene smiled. "I know they can't be ruled out until they are ruled out, but...really?"

"Hey, they were out on their boat on the lake the same afternoon Lori was killed. We haven't ruled them out because we can't yet. The professor was on the lake the same time in your rental boat and your creepy neighbour was out on the lake in his boat the same afternoon too. The boys were picked up by him at the dock, remember? So, they were in the area the same afternoon too. Ashley said she was hiking, but she was alone and no one can vouch for her either."

"Yeah, and I was working alone at the back shed clearing up the old roofing and no one saw me either don't forget."

"Sam saw you at times. You saw Sam around the property at times during the afternoon. You both alibi each other...somewhat. I guess Sam could have killed Lori and stuffed her into the kayak or you could have, and the boat on the lake with a man and a woman towing a kayak never even happened or had nothing to do with the murder. I know Sam though and he's not a likely suspect. Nor are you," Sarah added quickly.

"Phew!" Charlene said with another exaggerated eye roll. "Hey, why did you say creepy neighbour?"

"James got the creeps when he was talking to him. He got

the impression the guy was hiding something in his cottage. He blocked James' view and didn't let him in. James said he practically pushed him back out onto the deck when he opened the patio slider and James picked up some bits of blue rope from the guy's dock. You know, the same kind of rope we found tied around Lori's hands. It's pretty standard cheap rope that a lot of people use, but James bagged it anyway."

"What does he have to say about where he was that afternoon?" Charlene asked.

"He told us he was out on his boat for a few hours before he picked up the boys at your dock at the parking lot and took them to the dock at cottage #1 then went to his place. We don't have any grounds for a search warrant and Officer Edwards knows we can't use the rope as evidence without a warrant, but it was enough for us to try to get the guy to come into the station for an interview."

"And...," Charlene prompted hoping Sarah would tell her more. "Am I living across from a murderer or what?"

"He refuses to come in to the station, so we can't rule him out. We're going to try just going over to his cottage again and see if he will talk to us there, you know, routine canvassing stuff or something. If we can find where Lori was killed I'm hoping we'll find more evidence and be able to rule out some suspects. It's like an Agatha Christie novel right now, with everyone a suspect. The professor says he heard another boat on the lake but didn't actually see it. Sam said he saw a boat he is positive was Joe's boat, with a man sitting at the back running the motor and a woman at the front of the boat, and they were towing a yellow kayak. He also said he heard other boats but didn't see them from where he was painting. The Porters said when they were fishing they saw another fishing boat from a distance with only one person in it but they don't know if it was a man or a woman. Ashley told us she didn't see or hear any boats from where she was hiking or lost for a bit. The boys said the only boat they saw was your neighbour when he picked them up.

"This is all going on the premise that the suspect had a boat at all. Someone could have killed Lori near the resort and somehow then stuffed her into the kayak. That would explain no one seeing a boat launch the day she was killed. It's only Sam's statement that makes us look at a fishing boat since it sounds like he saw the killer. It adds up...the boat, the man, the woman with long hair and the kayak. But, the suspect could have come from land and that includes all the same people again. They could have easily pulled their boats up on shore somewhere and walked to the resort and killed Lori. Ashley could have walked back and killed Lori. This whole scenario includes anyone and everybody and I can't bear to think that." Sarah's shoulders slumped as she seemed to take in what she just said.

"That scenario puts Sam and me back on the list of suspects too. Seriously though, if the killer came by land then you'd think Sam or I would have seen the suspect at the canoe rack. That would take a lot of effort and time to get Lori's body from cottage #2 and placed in my kayak. It looked like she struggled too so I'm sure we would have heard something. I was working far back from the cottages for a few hours though and Sam was back and forth to the shed that's pretty close to that cottage but he usually puts on the radio pretty loud and closes the door while he's in the shed. And, the kayak was wet. How did it get wet if it wasn't in the water? I didn't take it out earlier," Charlene said.

"No but everyone told me Greg took it out without your permission a few times. You said he took your paddle from the office without asking. The professor told me he warned Greg about taking your kayak or canoes out again without your permission. He could have taken it out when the guys came back from the field day early."

"Yes but then Haiden and Peter would be at cottage #1 right in front of the canoe rack and would have seen Greg take it and seen him with Lori."

"That's assuming again Staff. Peter and Haiden could have had a nap or had their heads in their school stuff and not seen anything or worse case, be covering for Greg."

"When I put the canoes back with the professor, the guys were out front by the picnic table and there were beer bottles out. I think they were all drinking together after an early return from the field, playing truant since the professor was out in the fishing boat."

"Anyway, we're working hard Staff. We're going over the interviews and we've had follow-up interviews and checking everyone's statements against the others' etc. You know the drill. On another note, before you get me blabbing too much more, when are you going to Nova Scotia?"

"I don't know now, with this happening. I was thinking of November before the weather and roads get too bad. Everything is finished with the lawyer, so all I have to do is go there. He mailed me the key with the paperwork. I have a few new pictures the insurance guy sent to me. He went out there to see if it could be insured. Want to see them?"

"Sure. Anything right now would be a good diversion, even looking at pictures on someone's cell." Sarah smirked.

"Yeah, I know it's like watching someone's home movies."

"Home movies?"

"Oh yeah you're too young to know anything about those, lucky you. Anyway...here is a picture of the outside of the house."

"Gee Staff, I know I'm pretty new at this detecting stuff but I think I could have figured that out myself. Seeing the outside of the house would have been my first clue." Sarah ducked as Charlene threw one of the chair cushions at her.

"It's pretty old looking and looks like it will suck all the money out of your account. Are you sure about this?" Sarah asked with a look of disdain as she scrolled the cell screen.

Not only did Sarah not cook, she did not do house repairs. Patty ran the house and Sarah, well, Charlene wasn't sure what Sarah did at home. Patty and Sarah got along great though it seemed, so something must be working between them.

"Hey stop that. You're not supposed to look at someone's pictures without asking." Charlene laughed and tried to grab her phone.

"What is this a picture of?" Sarah asked, all the smile gone from her face as she stopped scrolling, cell phone held toward Charlene.

"Pass me the phone. Oh, those are those glasses Jack turned in. Remember, you saw them on the counter. I was going to send the picture in to the paper but changed my mind and the radio bit worked so fast I didn't need to. I just forgot to delete that picture."

Sarah pulled her phone out of her small black leather MEC back pack she always carried, on or off the job, and scrolled quietly, then turned her phone toward Charlene.

"Check this out."

Charlene took the phone and looked at a picture of Lori standing at a bar. It looked like she was smiling at someone beside her. Her face was to the side, not looking at the camera.

"Is this the Black Cat?" she asked.

"Yup. That's the picture the professor took and sent to me."

"It doesn't seem she's aware he took the picture."

"No but not just that. Look at it again."

Charlene used her finger tips to enlarge the photo on the screen. She looked up at Sarah and the colour drained from her face.

"You have my permission to scroll," Sarah said. "There's another more close-up picture of Lori that Ashley sent me."

"Oh man," Charlene said.

"Man oh man is right. Lori is wearing the same glasses that Jack turned in."

CHAPTER 48

Charlene

After Sarah left the office and walked over to cottage #5 to see if Jack and Edna were at the cottage, Charlene checked the time. She had time before the students would be back. She would take Officer Edwards over to the landing the same time she picked the students up and hopefully Officer Miller would be there too for a lift over. Sarah may be awhile talking to the Porters if they were even back. She heard a boat coming close to the resort while she and Sarah were having tea, and it sounded like her rental Yamaha, but she didn't look out.

Now would be a good time to eat a bit. She picked up some homemade bread from the general store on her way back and was hankering for a peanut butter and honey sandwich with lots of butter on the gooey white bread. Stacy seemed a lot more at peace then the last time Charlene saw her. Maybe living alone was agreeing with her and she'll be happier without Bill.

She felt hungry now that she was certain that Joe would be in the clear. Mr. Blake said Joe was in his shop around noon.

Now if he could only place Joe in his shop for the next few hours then there would be no way Joe could drive to the resort, launch his boat, take her kayak, pick up Lori, kill her somewhere and put her into the kayak, get the kayak on the rack, take his boat off the lake then drive home. She knew for some of that day he didn't have his own motor on his boat, but for how long?

Charlene had come back the day Lori was killed and saw Lori and Ashley around 1:00 o'clock. The boys and the "creepy" neighbour across the lake both say the boys were at the parking lot about 3:00 or 3:30 pm and as far as Charlene knew they stayed at the cottage. They certainly didn't take any of her boats out. They didn't ask to take any of her boats out was all she really knew for sure. They could have taken her kayak down and killed Lori and put her back. All three of them together? No, not a likely scenario she didn't think, and the other two would see if one of them killed her and was messing about at the canoe rack. The Scottish canoeists didn't get back until about 5:00 o'clock. She just happened to be walking down from the back of the property when she heard them out on the lake talking and saw them paddling toward the beach. She was heading back to check on the time to get the boys for 5:00 o'clock. When she got to the beach to greet the canoeists, she saw the boys were out by their picnic table. So, Lori was killed between 1:00 o'clock and 5:00 o'clock she knew for sure, but likely killed earlier since the boys were back by 3:30.

The professor showed up about 5:00 o'clock, so he was out on the lake all day alone as far as she knew, but he could have come back while she was working out back. He had no one to give him any alibi.

Sam was on the property with her all day. He still had the time to kill Lori with Charlene out back working. She knew he was no killer though. No way. Not Sam.

CHAPTER 49

Charlene

Still no word from Joe. Charlene wasn't going to leave another message. He let her know he was out of town, but not where he was, she thought, as she felt the anger rising. At least the police in Hamilton are going to ask him about that guy's motor repair. If only the time could all be accounted for then Joe would no longer be a suspect.

She took a sip of her whisky, as she sunk lower in the soaker tub. She poured herself an ounce of the only single malt whisky distilled in North America. She visited the Glenora Distillery on a drive to Cape Breton that spring when she went to Nova Scotia to look at the old house and decided she would buy it. The drive from the house was beautiful along the curvy, hilly road beside the eastern shore through quaint and subtle towns like Hadleyville, Sand Point, Pirate Harbour, Mulgrave, and into Auld's Cove and over the Canso Strait to Port Hastings, the entry point onto Cape Breton Island.

She took the tour of the small distillery and inn and got a

sample taste of the 10-year-old whisky, learning that it was not called Scotch only in that it was not distilled in Scotland. She stopped off at the liquor store outside of Port Hood on the way back to the old house and bought a bottle of Fiddler's Choice, the distillery tribute to a Cape Breton fiddler, John MacDougall who played and taught traditional fiddling on Cape Breton Island. The almost $60.00 price tag stopped her, but only briefly, before she thought it only fitting that she bring home a bottle of the local crafted whisky. Charlene stopped drinking beer and wine years before, the alcohol going to her head even after just sips. She poured the whisky, neat, into the little Irish pottery cup she bought at a flea market outside of Victoria on a trip to British Columbia. The ounce of precious liquid was warmed by her hands wrapped around the little tumbler. She liked that the whisky and tumbler had traveled across Canada reminding her of both coasts, one mild with not much snow, and the other cold and wild, but affordable for her. In a few years it would be her only home when she sold the resort and retired.

Whisky was a drink she could sip for a long time and with it came a quiet chance of contemplation, not impairment. The alcohol tingled her lips as she tried to conjure up the smell and taste of the water of MacLellan's brook, the source of water for the whisky, running through an old apple orchard and maple trees in Glenville known as 'The Glen' in the hilly terrain of Inverness County.

It had taken her years of trying to get the hang of whisky. After reading so many books with characters sitting in the tub after a busy, hard day sipping the drink, she was determined to make whisky her drink too. For some reason in the past year she just started to enjoy the taste of the wee dram, called by a former police colleague as 'nectar of the gods.'

Charlene swooshed the bubbles up around her, covering her body with the heady lavender smell. The whisky and the scent was calming her. She smiled as she thought of Officer Miller at her parking lot, not there to relieve Officer Edwards since Sarah released the area as a crime scene, but to meet Sam. Charlene took Sam over after the long day he spent painting exterior doors of some of the cottages and re-staining all the picnic tables. Wendy stepped out of her car as Sam stepped off the boat. She waved at Charlene and walked over to Sam's car and they both got in. Sam drove off, leaving Wendy's car in the lot, but not before turning toward Charlene with what Charlene thought was his version of a small smile. Well, well, she thought. Good for them.

I should make her pay for parking, thought Charlene, as she took another sip. The car was still there, the last time she looked when she picked up the students about 8:00 o'clock, a bit later than expected and in the dark.

Charlene recapped her day like usual. She found it made it easier to organize and file away details in her head in case she needed to recall something later. After eating two large sandwiches and a tall glass of milk, Charlene worked at raking up some of the pine needles along the paths between the cottages while waiting for the students to arrive. Sarah had some good luck when speaking to Jack and Edna and Charlene was going to take them out on the pontoon boat the next morning to see if they could locate the island where they found the glasses. They were certain they could.

Sarah told Charlene she thought they must be Lori's glasses, though how that could explain the young woman claiming them as hers was not yet figured out. Sarah didn't want to stay to work out that puzzle. She had a long night ahead of her at the station before coming back around 8:00 o'clock the next morning.

Everyone was accounted for. The Porters were in their cottage. The students, including Ashley, looked like they were hard at some course project. So much for Ashley not going near Greg. She never did find out what she meant when she yelled at the professor when Lori's body was found. Rocks and lots of charts and notes were strewn about the table in cottage #1. Paper was taped to the front windows. Charlene knew it would be hard to clean the bits of tape and sticky residue left on the glass. The students did it every year. She was going to ask Dan to tell them not to do it but forgot every year. Charlene had walked over to the cottage to check to see if they needed any more fire wood. She figured they were getting low, but they said they had enough and barely looked at her before getting their collective noses to the rock samples again.

As she walked back to the office, she thought she saw Dan sitting in his front porch. She heard the tinkling of ice. She waved in his direction and thought she saw him wave back. It was hard to tell even with the little porch light on.

The couple in cottage #4, were sitting out on their front screened-in porch. Charlene could see wine glasses in their hands as she said goodnight to them when she passed by in

A KAYAK FOR ONE

front of them on the path. They had come into the office after taking the canoe back to the Porters' dock, delighted with their outing, chatting to Charlene about what they saw on the lake. They left holding hands and went into the cottage and Charlene did not hear them come out again.

After Charlene locked up the office, she got her bath ready, and slipped into the tub with drink in hand and tried to make sense of the past few days.

CHAPTER 50

Saturday September 26th, 2015

Charlene

"That's it. That's where we stopped to have our picnic," Edna pointed to the small island, set among several other islands affording great privacy from most of the big part of the lake.

Charlene inched the pontoons forward after seeing a natural shallow, sandy, beach, just perfect for putting the boat to shore. Officer Edwards and Officer Phil Henderson, SOCO trained, were in one of her rental fishing boats. The police boat was in use out on the nearby lakes with an officer checking fishing licences. Officer Miller had a day off. Her car, Charlene noticed, was still at the landing. Sam phoned at 7:30 in the morning and asked if it was okay if he came in later to paint. She hoped Sam knew what he was doing. He was a sensitive guy who took his single-parent situation pretty seriously. Maybe that's it, she thought. He was taking his parenting seriously and just having a fling. He needs that too. Wendy did say she was checking out house prices around

Espanola, so maybe she was ready to settle in the area. With the O.P.P. though, she could be transferred anywhere in Ontario in a flash. Where would that leave Sam?

Charlene didn't mind taking Jack and Edna with her, knowing they would only be needed a short time. If the police found anything they could be hours and hours and Charlene had guests to take care of. Renting the fishing boat to the police seemed like the best solution. Of course she had Sarah on board too.

She left a note on the office counter to let the guests in cottage #4 know she would be gone an hour or so, and they could help themselves to a canoe from the rack since the police tape had come down. Her own kayak was still at the police station. James forgot to throw it on his truck his last shift. Maybe she would just get it herself, Charlene thought. She was anxious to have it so she could use the kayak in the nice fall weather. She shuddered. She wondered if she could ever use it again. Though not generally creeped out by death, she was having a hard time with this one. It was probably because of what Sam told her he saw. Things had been going so well with Joe. She wondered how she could carry on as usual with him again once he was cleared. She wouldn't be able to she knew. He didn't tell her about going to Hamilton or that he would be at his ex's house. Something was up and nothing he wanted to share with her it seemed. He hadn't even called her since he left the message to say he'd be away.

"Staff. Staff!"

Charlene shook off her thoughts and looked over at Sarah who was waiting for Charlene to get off the boat. She pointed

201

out a tree in front to tie the bow rope. It was a perfect spot to tie off. The boat wouldn't drift off, anyway. There was little wind so far and the island was mostly tucked in out of any wind that could kick up soon, which it usually did on the lake like clockwork, starting about 11:00 o'clock, not dying down again until about 5:30 or 6:00 p.m. The rental boat fit nicely beside the pontoon boat and Officer Edwards tied it off to the side rail of the pontoon boat before stepping over the rail to board the front of the pontoon boat, only to step off again at shore.

"I can't get my shiny boots wet Ms. Parker!" he said.

Officer Henderson hopped over the side of the fishing boat into the shallow water making a point, Charlene guessed, showing the young officer what a rough and tough he was. She couldn't help but notice though that some water squelched out the side of his boot when he made it to the rock on shore. She would have opted to keep her boots dry like James too. There was nothing worse than working a long shift in wet leather police boots. The boots these officers were wearing were a combination of supposed water-proof material and leather, but looked to be no better quality than Charlene's old police boots that ended up feeling like slippers after six years of wearing them as a beat officer, the imprints of her feet and toes ingrained in the leather insole.

After Charlene dropped off the students and the professor, she picked up the police officers at the landing as prearranged and took them over to the resort to get them settled in the fishing boat before stopping to pick up the Porters at their dock. Charlene thought they would have just walked the 100 feet to the pontoon boat dock, but no, they were standing at the end of the dock like royalty. She was sure it must have been Edna's idea.

Edna had on a bright, flowery, long-sleeved shirt over lime green linen pants, and was wearing bright green linen pull-on flat shoes. She was wearing what one could only call an Easter bonnet. It looked like she was dressed to go painting plein air, or to go to a tea room or something, not take a windy boat ride to the middle of the lake to point out where they stopped for lunch out in the wilderness. Jack had on his fishing cargo pants, a short-sleeved tee shirt, and had his windbreaker in his hand. He saw Charlene look at Edna and must have caught what she was thinking. He gave a little smirk with a slight shrug of his shoulders before he hopped onto the boat.

Edna started to walk off the boat, hand outstretched toward Charlene. Sarah stopped her by saying, "Stop!" It worked, but not without an angry look from Edna. Jack smiled and sat facing the sun and closed his eyes.

"Do not leave the boat please Mrs. Porter. Are you certain this is the place you had lunch?"

"Yes. We pulled our boat up right here in this exact spot and used that same tree to tie up the boat. We walked up there." She pointed to the smooth rock surface up a bit from the shoreline that flattened out on top.

"There's a fire pit up there. We didn't light a fire since it was so warm that day, but we carried our little cooler and put our chairs up there on top. We walked around a bit to stretch and were amazed to see so many blueberry bushes on one little island."

"I guess that's why they call this Blueberry Island," Charlene said. She added as she realized Edna didn't appreciate her humour, "I've been told there was an island called that but have never been here."

"Really Staff? You love blueberries. I thought you would have found out where this was and come here," Sarah said.

Charlene knew the only way Sarah got her blueberries was after Patty picked them hunched over alone in the bush with Sarah sitting in the truck, working at her police files.

"I can't come this far in July to pick blueberries and leave the guests. I can go up the back trail after the office closes for a half hour or so, but I'm too busy to take the time away to pick any longer. I get a little container each time. If I picked here though, I could pick enough at one to put in the freezer for the year!"

Sarah and the other two officers grabbed the police equipment bags from the deck of the pontoon boat. Charlene was ready to step onto shore when Sarah told her to stay where she was too. Edna looked pleased but had the grace to look away when Charlene looked back at her.

From where she was sitting, something fluttering near the tree caught Charlene's attention. She walked to the front of the boat and walked out over the pontoon, careful not to touch land and suffer the ire of Sarah. She knew she shouldn't walk on the island anyway. Since it was where the glasses Jack turned in were found, the whole island would be a crime scene. It would have to be treated as one anyway until otherwise. Charlene still didn't get why Sarah was fixated on the glasses as Lori's. The rightful owner already picked them up. She described them to the finest detail before Charlene took the glasses over to the landing to give to her. Sure they were exactly the same as the ones Lori was wearing in the pictures at the pub that night, but.. But what? Charlene thought. Same pair of glasses on two women on the same lake? Yeah. She could see how Sarah was thinking it was too weird. Sarah practically kissed her before she left the office to talk to the Porters, after she saw the picture of the glasses on her cell phone. Well, she did in fact kiss her. Full on the mouth. An attempt at a lingering kiss if Charlene was not mistaken. She may have to be careful with her.

She could see that it was a small length of blue rope tied to the same cedar tree she tied her rope to, just under one of the boughs. It looked like it had been cut at one end. The other end looked like it had been burned to stop it from fraying. She knew the rope. It was cheap rope that she saw a lot of cottagers use on their boats. She bought it once to tie down a tarp over the Muskoka chairs in front of the office for winter. The rope didn't hold up to the ice and snow and fell apart in her hands when she untied it in the spring. She learned to buy good marine rope after that for all her boat lines and any outside project, so she knew the blue rope did not come from Jack and Edna's rental boat when they moored on the island. She remembered the blue rope tied around Lori's wrists and that Officer Edwards found small blue strands on her neighbour's dock across the lake.

She snapped a picture of it with her cell phone. It reminded her of a murder of a young woman, a girl from a farm, new to the big city, a McMaster University student. Her ex-boyfriend walked into her dorm room, with her roommate there too, and pulled out a shotgun from under the long coat he was wearing and shot the woman he did not want to lose. The first patrol officer to arrive was there quickly, but so were the paramedics, working on the young woman in a futile attempt to save her life after being shot at full blast from only a few feet away.

The officer knew the crime scene was being contaminated with the rush of the paramedics and firefighters on scene and the hysterics of the roommate running about the room. He saw a camera in the room and started taking pictures of the victim and of the room from every angle. He gave the camera to the detectives who arrived later to take over the investigation. This was before cell phones were small enough to put in a uniform shirt pocket. The pictures on the developed film proved to be valuable to the investigation and the officer was praised for his quick thinking. The victim's body had been removed from the room and rushed off in hopes of resuscitation so the detectives had to rely on the snap shots to figure out what happened to prove the case in court. It was awful for them though, since the film had snap shots of the victim with friends and family and her ex-boyfriend, looking happy, very much alive, mixed in with shots of her body on the floor with the fatal damage from the shotgun blasts. Charlene never forgot that case and used her camera, now her cell phone, on instinct, especially when involved in police investigations.

She would tell Sarah when she came back to the boat. She looked back at Edna. She had her nose in a book she pulled out of her handmade cloth bag she carried everywhere. She doubted Edna was reading. There's no way she would want to miss this. Jack's eyes were still closed and she thought she saw a twitch on his cheek. How he could be so relaxed living with Edna was a surprise to her.

Charlene could see Phil walk quickly from the flat area by the fire pit to his equipment bag. He rummaged around for a few seconds then walked back to the pit and pulled something from the ashes and put it into what looked like an evidence bag. He took his pen from his uniform pocket and spent a minute filling in the label before sealing the bag. He set the bag into his pant leg cargo pocket then took out his notebook and spent a moment writing. Charlene figured he was making note of whatever he found, where he found it, and the police report number for the Forensic Unit in Orillia or The Centre for Forensic Science in Toronto. He went back to his bag and pulled out a square piece of mesh and began sifting through the ashes. Sarah walked up to him and crouched beside him. Charlene couldn't hear what they were saying, but knew something important had been found. She could see James walking slowly around the edge of the small island, using his baton to pull back the brush and the branches of the blueberry bushes. Sarah stood up and walked toward the pontoon boat.

"Okay Staff. You may as well head back with the Porters. We'll be here for awhile. I'll be fine. James will help me into the boat and I will be okay for the short trip back."

"Look Sarah. Text me when you are finished. If I'm available I'll come get you," Charlene answered.

"Thanks. I'll see."

The look of relief on Sarah's face would make the extra trip back worthwhile. Charlene would hate to see her suffer. Her phobia about being in small boats was real to her.

"Before I go Sarah...," Charlene said as she pointed to the piece of blue rope tied to the tree.

She watched Sarah's face as she looked at the rope. Her face went from puzzlement to understanding before the smile spread across her face, erasing some of the stress lined between her eyes. If the Porters weren't there she probably would have pumped her fists in the air.

"We are here Staff," she whispered, looking over at Edna who was leaning forward on her chair watching them.

"This is the crime scene. I'm positive. There's a piece of fishing line in the fire pit. It hasn't been burned and there is something on it, blood I'm hoping. It looks like spots of blood on the ground beside it on the flat rock. We're closer to getting the bastard. Phil! Bring the camera and an evidence bag."

As Phil came running Jack snorted and opened his eyes.

"I'm coming back with you now Staff. Our visit to your neighbour has been moved up to now. I'll get Wendy to meet me at the landing and come with me."

"She may be at the landing already. Her car was still there when we left. I guess you didn't notice it, oh great detective," Charlene smirked. "Sam will have to drop her off at her car anyway when he comes to paint this morning, if he hasn't already."

"Sam?"

"I'll tell you later."

CHAPTER 51

"I need to see your boat and fishing licence and your emergency safety equipment."

Geez, was the guy stupid or something. It was the third time O.P.P. Officer Allan Fisher told the guy and the third time the guy just stared at him. Was he deaf or something? Oh, shit, he thought, maybe he was.

Before he could try to mime what he wanted, the guy sitting in the fishing boat answered him.

"Sorry officer. I must have been daydreaming," he said as he opened his tackle box and lifted the top layer.

"Here's my fishing licence, and here's my boat operator licence."

"Daydreaming of the big one that got away, eh?" Officer Fisher said as he reached from the police boat to get the licence.

"Maybe the one that didn't get away," the guy said with a loud laugh.

As Officer Fisher studied the licences he noticed the guy was fidgeting with some fishing line that was loose in the tackle box.

He saw him looking and said, "It's a mess. I guess I better buy some new stuff. It's all tangled."

"I guess you better buy an anchor while you're at it," Officer Fisher said pointing to the front of the boat. A blue line was tied to the bow of the boat and hung down into the boat, a few feet long.

"I have one here," he replied, said lifting a big rock tied to good yellow and blue marine rope on the floor of the boat beside his seat. It was tied to the handle on the outside of the boat at the back.

"At least you have better rope there than at the front. That blue line is useless. What happened? Did it just break while you had your anchor in?"

"Yeah, something like that."

"Okay then. I see your baler."

Officer Fisher smiled at the old bleach bottle with the end cut out that a lot of boaters used. They made good balers actually, he thought, with the handle at the other end and the bottom cut out like a scoop. It would be better than the stupid little orange container that contained the rest of the boating emergency kit that he used in his own fishing boat.

"Have you got a flashlight, whistle and rope?" he asked.

"Yup," the guy said as he crouched forward to get off the life jacket he was using as a seat cushion. He reached into the front pocket and pulled out the small LED flashlight. The whistle was attached to the life jacket.

"I've got lots of line on this anchor," he added, pointing to the rock.

"Okay. Yeah, okay, that's good." Officer Fisher was

content to leave the guy in peace. It was a gorgeous sunny day and he was assigned to spend his shift in the police boat checking for fishing and boating licences and liquor infractions.

He had just come back from two weeks of vacation, spent with family in Hamilton and he was glad to be back in the north and out on the water. He was hoping to get out on his own boat for a bit after work. His wife couldn't deny him that after he agreed to being in the city with her parents for all of his summer vacation.

He looked at the licence again before passing it back.

"Okay thanks," he said, noticing the local address. "I hope you catch some. I've been told the bass have really been biting."

"Yeah they are. I'm on this lake a lot. It's close to motor over and dock behind the pub. Not for beer!" he said when he saw the look on the officer's face, "the chicken wings!"

Officer Fisher started the police boat. He looked at his watch. It would be dark soon and his shift was almost over. He made his way to the dock. As he pulled away he looked back. The guy pulled at the motor and put it into gear. With a wave in his direction he moved off down the shoreline trolling, probably hoping for a big bass in the shallow weeds. Officer Fisher was glad the guy wasn't far from the dock either. His motor was missing every few seconds and seemed like it might conk out on him.

CHAPTER 52

Charlene

"Sorry Charlie. I meant to bring it back a few days ago."

The professor held the box of fishing line out for Charlene to take.

"I put it on the reel, but didn't catch anything so I took it off again and got it back in the box."

He put the fishing rod against the office counter.

"I like this light-weight rod. With the heavier line it would have been fun to catch a big bass and test both the rod and line. I was lucky to watch a porcupine for a long time though. It was huge. It was on the shoreline right in front of the boat, eating the weeds at shore. I got some great pictures on my new digital camera. I'll send you some when I get back to good internet."

"Thanks Dan."

Charlene put the box of line back into the drawer. Why does everyone send her pictures of the lake and the resort when they get home? She wondered. She felt like yelling at them sometimes. 'I live here! Remember?!' Oh well, they get excited and they keep coming back and she gets excited when she sees her bank balance and the retirement house in Nova Scotia becomes more of a reality. No. Not just that, she thought. She liked when guests got excited about nature. She did too.

Dan lingered in the office, not talking, just looking at her.

"Are you okay Dan?"

"Yeah. Maybe. No."

"Do you want a coffee? I've had a busy day today with the police and everything and missed my coffee this morning. I shouldn't have caffeine this late in the day but I really would like one anyway," Charlene offered."

"Yes, thanks, I would. I'd like to talk to you about something if you have time," Dan said.

"Of course. I'll put the coffee on and be back down in about 15 minutes."

"Can I just sit in here and wait?"

"Sure just tell anyone who comes in to ring the outside doorbell to get my attention so you don't have to yell up at me."

Charlene put the dark roast coffee in the percolator. She set it on the stove and went into the bathroom. She was shocked to see herself in the mirror. Her fair hair was dull and she had dark circles under her eyes. Her eyes looked sick, the ring around the gray iris darker than normal. She had a pimple near the side of her mouth. A pimple at this age was not fair, she thought. Her work pants were hanging off her. She felt weaker as she looked at herself. The skin on her upper arms showing beneath the sleeves of her tee shirt was saggy. Oh man. Gravity sucks, she thought. She knew she better get back at yoga and Pilates and weights. Stress and age were taking a toll. She washed her face and put her hair up in a small bun at the back. Her hair was just long enough to get it off her neck at least. She reached for her mascara then thought Dan would notice and that was not a message she wanted to send. He didn't seem to notice how worn she looked or didn't seem to care anyway.

She turned the stove down and took some peanut butter cookies out of the freezer and put them on a plate. She baked them a few weeks before when she had a quiet morning. When the coffee was ready she set everything on the tray set with sugar and cream in case Dan wanted to dress up his coffee.

It was already 5:30. How did that happen? She spent the better part of the day cleaning up more pine needles from in front of the cottages along the path, knowing the morning dew made for a slippery walk if she didn't keep at it. The day had been beautiful but the forecast was for cooler temperatures the next day and some rain overnight. She was hoping for a storm so she could lay in bed and watch the lighting. It had been hot enough lately for a good night show. She wanted the sky to be clear the next night for the lunar eclipse though.

After dropping off the Porters and Sarah, Charlene kept herself busy so she wouldn't think of Joe. She spent a few hours at cleaning up the property, raking and piling the needles for Sam to take to the back bush with the ATV and trailer. She went into the storage area beside the office and took most of the linen out of closest and put the washed sheets into clear plastic bags for the winter. She did the same with the dish towels and spare bath towels. She wiped down the shelves and was content that she made a good start to the tedious task of winterizing. It wouldn't be long before the resort would be closed for the season. She could almost taste the relief, knowing her time would be her own for the most part once the resort was put to bed after Thanksgiving. She wouldn't have to keep checking e-mail and phone messages so much. Guests called in the winter to book for the summer, so she had to keep on top of it, but it wasn't so hectic. A lot of people told her how lucky she was that she had all winter off. Like most resort owners, the start-up began by the end of March to get the cottages ready and ended around November, when all the cottages were put to bed for the season. Working 12 hour days and having to be at-the-ready the rest of the time every day for so many months with no days off was physically and emotionally draining. All in all, her days off in the winter probably added up to fewer than the nights and week-ends most people had away from work. There was no telling them that though. They just didn't get it just like people who have never worked night shift can fully get what it feels like to work when so many others are sleeping, then try to sleep when so many people are mowing lawns, using leaf blowers, talking loudly and just living life. Her eyes grew heavy at the thought of sleep and rest.

Sam had a busy day painting the rest of the exterior cottage doors and a couple of porch floors before hauling the piles of needles away. He smiled at her a few times, more smiles than she had seen from him since she first hired him. There was no need for words with Sam though, so nothing was said. They kept busy all day, until she took him over to the landing when it was time to get the students at 5:00 o'clock. She was glad she took the chance around 4:00 o'clock to stretch out on the hammock strung between two old, towering white pines in front of the office close to the lake. The couple from cottage #4 were out in the canoe all day, so she wouldn't disturb them. The hammock was close to the door to the screen porch of that cottage and when there were guests there Charlene was careful to stay clear and allow the guests privacy. To her, 4:00 o'clock was the best time to watch the lake. The sunlight hit the small waves and the lake filled with diamond dapples. The sunshine hit her face and calmed her. The upstairs of the house was amazing the same time of day too, as the big stained glass window in the living room caught the sunlight and spread the colors of the glass all over the walls and ceiling, mixing in with the moving patterns of sunlight reflected off the lake.

Dan was working on the jigsaw puzzle she kept out on the long pine harvest table under the office window. Guests were welcome to sit and work at the puzzle while the office was open. She had to kick guests out many times when she wanted to lock up for the day. The doorbell was for guests for after hours. If in the house, Charlene could just walk out to the front balcony and look over to see what they needed. Many times they just wanted back in to work on the puzzle. She let them in and locked the office door again and asked them to let her know when they left so she could lock up again. She wasn't concerned about the office desk and computer being in the same room behind the counter or the cash register. She always locked up the register after she closed the office, taking any great sums of money out. This time of year there was little cash. Most people paid with debit or credit cards anyway. She brushed away the thought of all the bank fees she had paid this season and before it could set her teeth on edge, she set the tray down on the table by the wood stove.

They both sat down in the big pine chairs cushioned with down and covered with remnants of an old Hudson Bay blanket Charlene sewed into cushion covers. Facing each other, not saying anything for a few minutes, they sipped their coffee.

"This is pretty embarrassing for me Charlie. What I want to tell you is shameful really but it is eating away at me. I understand if you don't want to listen now that I've said that," Dan said, looking down at the floor.

Charlene was sure now that she wanted to hear what he had to say. Was he going to confess to killing Lori? Her nerves were on edge.

"I put my arm around Ashley and tried to kiss her a couple of nights after we arrived."

Ashley? Charlene wondered. What the hell.

"The others were in the cottage doing clean-up duty after dinner and Ashley and I were sitting by the fire alone. I took a chance and it backfired. To be fair," he said when he saw the look on Charlene's face, "she came on to me at one of the pub nights when we got together as a group to make plans for this trip. Yeah, I know, it seems weird, a man my age, but it's true Charlie, I swear. The others left us alone at the pub table and she was rubbing up against me and saying suggestive things. I thought she was interested so that's why I put my arm around her."

Dan stopped to watch Charlene's reaction. Seeing a blank face and non-judgmental expression, he carried on.

"She was disgusted and told me she would report me to the university when we got back. I'll probably lose my job. Thinking about it, I probably should."

If he was looking to her as an ally he was barking up the wrong tree, she thought.

"The thing is, that I have a lot of debts with my divorce settlement and I still need to work. I've never done this before in all my years teaching. This seemed different though. I don't know why. Anyway, it's too late. She said she would continue with the course then report me when we are back. She knows the value of this course on her resume. After Lori was killed, Ashley has been acting really strange. She yelled at me and Greg when Lori's body was discovered, remember? I thought I was the only one who knew why she yelled at me. I guess she yelled at Greg because she made it seem as though he killed Lori. After the police came she said she was leaving. She has since changed her mind, obviously, and is sticking it out. She talks to Greg and Peter and even Haiden now and is almost pleasant to be around. Almost. She scares me Charlie."

"Scares you how?"

"Well just the way she changed her mind so much and the way she looks at me. She even told me she wasn't going to report me. I don't know if I feel sicker with her telling me that or being reported. Something's not right with her. The thing is though I've found out that all the others know that I tried to kiss her. Peter told me that Greg was standing at the kitchen window washing dishes and looked out just as I put my arm around her. He told Lori. I guess you know he and Lori used to be a couple, and it seems he still wanted to continue the relationship but she broke it off. Lori told Ashley that they all saw her hitting on me that night in the pub. She denied it and she and Lori got into a big argument. She said she would never go for a guy my age and was adamant she would report me.

"The morning that Lori and Ashley were sick and didn't come with us out in the field, the day we found Lori's body, Greg went into their cottage to get them moving and heard them still arguing. Lori called Ashley a slut and that set her off and she went for Lori, pushing her against the counter in their cottage. After Lori was killed, Greg told Peter and Peter told me. Peter's been close to Greg since the murder, worried he might go off the deep edge or something, but Peter felt he should tell me." Dan stopped to drink some coffee. He was clearly shaken. "By the way, did you know Peter was gay?"

"No," she said, but yes she thought. How did Dan not notice how Peter looked at Greg and not the girls?

"Yeah he is. He told me he lives with a guy in London. While at Brock he's in a shared apartment with another student from our course who couldn't make this trip. He said she's great to live with since she knows he's gay. His partner is at Western. He's going to be a dentist. Maybe he can use the gold Peter finds to fill his patients' teeth.

"Anyway, Ashley was here that day remember? She said she was sick but then she went off into the woods and told us later she got turned around. Remember?"

"I remember," Charlene nodded, seeing where he was going with this.

"She could have killed Lori and stuffed her into that kayak and no one was here. You come and go and your other guests are always out in their boat. I was out in the rental boat that day, and the guys were out in the field. Your neighbour picked them up about 3:30 they said. That left a lot of time for Ashley to kill her."

"I was back by 1:00 o'clock and saw both girls alive, at their cottage steps and I saw you about 5:00 o'clock when the canoe group came back," she said.

"I remember that," Dan said. "I was nowhere near the resort with the boat all day though, until I brought the boat back."

"Maybe that explains something," Charlene said. "She was talking to me about that night in the university pub and how everyone went off to follow Lori after Ashley called her a snob. She seemed to have remembered something and that's when she told Detective Davidson she changed her mind and was going to stay here. Did she have so much to drink that she could have a blackout?"

"Maybe. She drinks a lot. You're thinking she forgot that she came on to me?"

"Maybe. It seemed that way to me now that I think about how she reacted in the middle of telling me about it. It seemed as though she just remembered something that made her look embarrassed."

"I know you don't have locks on any of the cottage doors

Charlie, but I did put a lock on the inside of the front door and I shove a chair against the back door at night. To tell you the truth, I'm scared. Did she kill Lori? Am I next?"

The doors into the screen porches of all the cottages had only a hook and eye lock on the inside, mainly to stop the doors from slamming open and closed in the wind. The door going into the cottage from the porch were all the old-fashioned tongue and groove pine boards with the iron latch that guests could lift up to open the door. Only a few guests complained about no lock on this door. She tried to assure them that she knew all her guests and kept an eye out for any stranger on the property, or any guest going into a cottage that wasn't theirs. Most were okay with this, but some thought it very odd that she was so trusting with their stuff. To those, she suggested they lock up any valuables in their car. To that, she only had one guest question how safe the cars were in the parking lot across the lake. She was glad she didn't have anything of real value anymore to care about and didn't care if anyone stole from her. People would steal if they were thieves, no matter what, and she wasn't about to get locks installed only to have to chase all the guests for the keys at check out or worry they would get them duplicated when in town. She knew people would lose them and she would have to have so many spare sets. It seemed easier to her to leave the place old-fashioned and try to create a sense of peace among all the guests and get them to chill out while away from the city life.

"I'll keep the lock off when we are gone for the day in case you need to get it into the cottage for anything. I better go and get the students organized for dinner. They are busy working on the assignment for today. They're working harder now. The course is almost finished and I'm worried about the future."

With that Dan put his mug on the tray, seemed to just notice the cookies, and took a few.

"For after dinner Charlie. Thanks for listening."

As they both stood up, he stepped closer to Charlene and hugged her hard and long. She believed everything he told her. She could feel it.

As he walked toward the door, Dan selected a piece of curly paper from the brightly coloured pottery bowl Charlene had on the counter.

He read aloud, "Your days brighten as your heart lightens."

He turned toward Charlene and smiled and she noticed the lines of stress had faded from his face.

"That is perfect," he said, as he put the paper back in the bowl among the handfuls of paper, each with notations of thought typed on them for guests to pick out at random if they chose.

As she started to walk back to the storage area to put her fishing rod away, she stopped dead. She walked back to the office and opened the drawer. She lifted up the box of fishing line. She read 330 yards. If it was all there then Dan didn't use any to kill Lori. Not this fishing line anyway. She was sure Dan was no killer. Where was her tape measure? No, she better call Sarah. She put the box into her locked filing cabinet.

CHAPTER 53

Bob

Bob saw them coming. That detective and the police woman. He was hanging his dish cloth on the deck railing to dry. It was starting to smell. All his clothes were starting to smell. His bedroom was starting to smell. He should have gone into Espanola and done his laundry.

It was too late to get back inside and pretend he wasn't there.

They saw him.

CHAPTER 54

Sunday September 27th, 2015

Charlene

"Thanks Stacey, I'll come in as soon as I can."

Charlene had run out of the bedroom to grab the phone thinking it was Joe. It was just Stacey from the store calling to say Charlene had a parcel from Purolator. Charlene turned on the coffee and got dressed for the day. It was raining. She must have slept soundly for a change. She didn't hear the rain start. It must have been the great Pilates she did before dinner, then the walk into the woods after dinner along the creek that meandered at the back of her property, cascading down the rocks along the edges. The flowing water and the growing plants constantly changed the landscape, and Charlene never tired of looking at it.

As soon as Dan left after their chat, she changed into her comfy pants and tank top and unrolled her mat. She really needed the exercise routine and she got away from it the past few days. After her workout, she had a chance to cook some beets from Mr. Blake. She opened a tin of chunk pineapples and heated them on the stove with some corn starch, stirring until the mixture thickened. When the beets had boiled long enough she drained the vibrant liquid into a glass measuring cup and put the small pieces of beets in with the pineapples to keep warm. She cooked some rice and put a large dollop on her plate and topped it off with the pineapples and beets and added a few green leaves from the beet tops as her salad on the side. She couldn't remember the name of the dish, but it was in her ancient red and white Better Homes and Gardens New Cook Book she'd had since the early 70s, the pages all gooey with butter and batter and sticking out, but all in order. The only page missing was 99/100, the one with a great cranberry loaf recipe. When the beet liquid cooled, she poured it into a glass and drank it down.

There was still enough light after dinner so she put on her jeans and a light jacket and walked into the woods. She needed it, the smell, the rawness, the natural beauty. She left a note on the office door and was gone for just a short time. When she came back everything looked in order and no one came running for her so she got into the shower and into bed.

When Charlene unlocked the office door the next morning, the young couple from cottage #4 were standing outside peering in the big window. They had their hands cupped around their faces pressed against the glass. Oh man, now what? Charlene thought. Toilet leaking? Mouse in the cottage? No toilet paper? It must be something for them to be out at 8:00 o'clock in the morning in the rain.

"Hi Charlie," they both said as she opened the door.

"Good morning. Everything okay?" she hoped.

They said they missed their kids so were ready to check out and head home. The rain was probably a deciding factor Charlene thought.

"Can you wait until I take the students over and come back? I was just heading out to do that," she said.

They left the office to get their bags ready and said they'd wait in the porch of the cottage out of the rain. Charlene walked down to the boat. The students came running from the cottages despite their good rain gear and Dan sauntered over, his Tilley hat dripping water from the rim down his back. He smiled at Charlene and she noticed he looked rested and at peace somehow. She couldn't help but look at Ashley on the way to the parking lot in a different light. Sarah was going to come over later in the day when she had a chance to leave the office.

Charlene got big hugs when the couple hopped onto the boat. They said they put the canoe gear in the cottage and returned the canoe to the rack. Charlene wasn't in the mood to say it would have to come off so she could check it before they left. She had the end of the season ennui. As soon as she got back from the landing, she got her laundry basket ready and went in to clean cottage #4.

As she ran back into the laundry area with the pile of laundry, Charlene was startled to see the Porters sitting in the office by the fire. She took off her raincoat and shook it out before going in to see them.

"What a day!" she said to them.

"We were so lucky with the weather the whole week," Edna said.

"Oh my God!" Charlene exclaimed. "I forgot you were checking out today! How could I forget that?! I am so sorry to keep you waiting."

"We saw your note that you were in cottage #4. We were happy to just sit by the fire. We've only been here a few minutes," Edna said as she stretched her legs out to the warmth from the wood stove.

"We were thinking that if the cottage was available we'd like to stay another few nights. You've been talking about that eclipse and since tonight is supposed to be the best night for viewing, we don't want to miss it. I have my tripod all set and ready to take to the dock if it clears up. Even if it doesn't, we'd like to stay longer."

"Yes it is available and it would be great to have you here longer and the forecast is for this mess to stop by mid-day," Charlene said, relieved she wouldn't have to clean their cottage today too.

She tried to clean the cottages as the guests left just in case someone showed up at the landing without a reservation. That happened often enough in the off seasons. If she had to leave a cottage not cleaned because she was just too busy, she at least cleaned out the garbage and took out the dirty linens. Anything less was too disgusting.

Edna looked at Charlene for a moment. Charlene thought she was checking to see if she was sincere. She tried to keep any negative thought of Edna out of her mind so it wouldn't reflect on her face. Jack was standing just to the side and slightly behind Edna as per his usual place, and gave Charlene the thumbs up sign behind Edna's back.

"I have been so busy with my photography and sketching, I'm afraid I haven't noticed that Jack has hardly had the time to go fishing."

Edna turned toward Jack and gave him a beatific smile. He stepped forward and put his arm around her shoulders.

"So we want to keep the boat too for the next few days and the rest of the holiday will be for Jack to fish when he wants," Edna said.

Man oh man, thought Charlene. Just when you think you have someone figured out they become nice right in front of your eyes. She didn't think much surprised her anymore, but seeing the Porters as a loving couple did.

"If you have another copy of that fishing book you gave Jack, I'd love to borrow it so I can understand what all the fishing fuss is about. Jack seems to have misplaced his."

CHAPTER 55

Charlene

"Hello again, Charlie," Mr. Blake greeted Charlene as though he hadn't just seen her a few days before. Maybe that's why she liked being around him. He really got excited around people.

"Hi Mr. Blake. Hi Stacey. Hey, thanks again for the beets. I had some last night and they were so good. Thanks Stacey," she said as Stacey passed her a small parcel and the paperwork to sign.

"Anytime Charlie. I just took a basket over to Joe this morning."

"Joe?"

"Yes. Joe, your fella'. I know he was away for a day, but don't tell me you forgot about him already!" he laughed and was still laughing when he said he better get moving so he didn't stiffen from the damp and not be able to get moving.

When Mr. Blake was out of the store, Stacey said, "Yes Joe is back. He came in just before I closed yesterday. He went to Bennett's market when he was in Hamilton and got me a basket of Northern Spy apples so I can bake some pies. He picked out a dozen for himself. I don't know why they are called 'Northern' when everyone knows you can hardly ever get them in the north."

Did everyone know he was in Hamilton? Charlene wondered. Did everyone but her know why he was in Hamilton and why he was at his ex's house?

"Did he say why he was in Hamilton Stacey?" Charlene asked knowing that whatever was said between them would stay between them.

"No, just that he had some unpleasant business to see to and that he was glad to be back. I think he's making you a cake Charlie. He bought some whipping cream and eggs to make an upside down apple cake that he said he would top with the cream. I asked him to bring me a piece if there's any left."

"Yeah right."

"That's what he said."

Charlene left the store in a daze. She knew Stacey noticed she was upset but was kind enough to keep quiet. She could feel the sickness in her stomach and her eyes started to burn. Tears would follow. She had to sit in her car for a minute before pulling away and driving home. What the hell was going on?

She got back to mist rising from the lake with the sun coming out stronger and no more rain. The view from the road going into the resort was amazing. She looked down at her cell and thought about getting out and taking a shot, but thought she would just let the image of the flat water, the mist, and the trees dripping with the reds and oranges of fall colour contrasted against the white rock at the shoreline soak into her mind...an image to be retrieved when she needed a moment of beauty. Like now, she thought. The beauty almost made her forget that Joe was back and he didn't call her.

She went into auto pilot and got onto the pontoon boat and slowly made her way back over to the resort. She tucked the small Purolator package into the top of her coat. The seats of the boat were still sopping wet. Everyone had to stand on the boat ride over to the landing in the morning and Charlene didn't like that. She had to go slowly so nobody would keel over.

After she docked the boat, Charlene went up to the shed to get an old towel and walked back to start the tedious task of drying all the stacking chairs. As she bent over the crunching sound in her coat reminded her she had a package in her coat. She took it out and opened it up. Inside the gorgeous lilac and silver wrapping paper was a beautifully crafted round porcupine quill box with the design of a beaver on the top of the lid. The bottom was signed by the artist, a local woman from Manitoulin Island. Charlene knew they cost hundreds of dollars. She looked at a display of such boxes in Turner's of Little Current on the island. She lifted the lid. Inside nestled in soft purple velvet was a note. As she opened the paper and read the words "I love you" written in Joe's hand, she turned to the sound of approaching footsteps.

"Hello Charlene."

"Hello Joe."

After the students were picked up and the office closed for the day, they worked side by side in the kitchen chopping celery, onions, a few chunks of sweet potato, tender peas and carrots and small pieces of beef. When the meat was browned in hot oil, they put everything into the big pot on the stove and added the cut up vegetables including whole, small, new white potatoes and lots of black pepper.

"When will dinner be ready?" Joe asked.

"That's the beauty of stew," Charlene said.

"It can stew."

"Yes."

CHAPTER 56

Charlene

Charlene hopped out of bed to the parking lot phone ringing. It was down in the office instead of upstairs where she usually put it in the evening. She threw her feet into her moccasins and ran down to answer the phone.

"Don't tell me you forgot about me Staff!"

"Okay I won't. Can you give me a few minutes?"

"I see Joe's car here."

Charlene could hear the smirk in her voice.

Charlene ran back up to get dressed. She looked at the clock on the stove as she passed the kitchen. It was 6:30 p.m. It would be dark soon, and for sure when she took Sarah back over. Joe was out of bed and getting dressed.

"It's Sarah. She told me she was coming today but when she didn't show up earlier I guessed it was off."

"How about you take me over to the landing when you get her and I will go home and come back around 9:00 o'clock. How about we then have a late, well-stewed mug of dinner then check out the eclipse?" Joe asked. "I didn't bring warm

233

enough clothes for sitting out in the night air, and I forgot something at home."

Charlene realized she didn't even see Joe's car parked in the lot when she got back from the store.

"By the way, how did you get over here when I was gone?" she asked Joe.

"I was at the dock and called over. I was just about to hang up the phone when your guest Jack came over in the fishing boat. He was bailing out the boat at the dock and saw me pull up. He said he saw you leave so came over to see who I was and what I wanted. He was doing sentry duty while you were gone."

"Ah that is so nice of him." Charlene loved having Jack at the resort. He was one of the nice guests.

"I was going to put my boat into the lake since the fish would really be jumping today with all the rain. I was thinking of putting it in closer to my house to really surprise you but had no idea my car parked in plain sight would do the same thing." Joe smiled and pulled on his rubber boots at the same time Charlene did.

"On this lake?"

"Of course this lake! How else could I have surprised you?"

"Where can you put your boat in this lake closer to your house?"

"On the road to the reserve. You know that dirt road that goes off the highway near the village? The one that has the private property sign a little way up the road?" he asked.

"Oh yeah. The private property road that I wouldn't think to drive up on since there is the huge private property keep out sign."

"It's not private property right at the start of the road. There's a natural spot to back the trailer into the lake and park the truck and trailer at the side of the road."

"I had no idea anyone could get on the lake without coming on my ramp or from one of the houses in Miner's Village," she said.

She realized the killer didn't have to be someone on the lake already. It could be an outsider or someone who lives in the area and knows about that launching spot.

CHAPTER 57

Charlene

"So, he's coming back later. I won't be long anyway. I've had a long day already and Patty is home so I should be there too," Sarah said in a manner that was clear she did not want to go home.

Charlene knew the feeling. For many officers the long hours and the heavy responsibility of solving a murder made home just a house to go to for sleep and food. The relationship with the family came second for the most part during a serious investigation and it was often better to stay late at the office to not provoke arguments or be the cause of misunderstandings while focusing on solving a case.

"Spill. You look better Staff. Not much, but a bit."

"Joe was in Hamilton at his ex's house for a few reasons. The main one was that she phoned him really upset at just finding out that their son's adoption papers were final and they were the legal parents of the little guy they had been fostering."

"That was upsetting to her?"

"It seems so. Stuart is gay and lives with Tony. They've been foster parents to a little boy for a year and the chance came up to adopt so they started the process. Now that it's over they are ecstatic. Joe's ex is screaming like a banshee. She hasn't accepted Stuart's life choice even though he's been openly gay for over a decade. He's 34 or something now, for Pete's sake. Joe said she won't even talk to Tony and they've been married for five years and were living together for a few years before that. I think the fact they own a flower shop on Locke Street is the icing on the cake for her." Charlene laughed.

Sarah laughed and said, "Oh man. A flower shop? Two gay guys? Tony? Italian? This just gets better and better!"

"I know, too funny eh? Well it seems Joe's ex, Brenda, is moving to Florida and wants to sell her house the same one that used to be their house. She knows how much Joe loved that old house in a great neighbourhood just around the corner from Locke Street. It was an old cottage or something, but Joe fixed it up and it's worth a lot of money now. She offered Joe a chance to buy the house from her again. I guess she needs money. Joe got really upset because of the way she was talking about Stuart and Tony. Instead of being excited about being a grandmother for sure now, she is really upsetting them. Simon is only two now so he doesn't understand all the commotion, but he will soon if she keeps it up."

"So is Joe going to buy the house?"

"He said not for him, but he knows Brenda won't sell it to Stuart knowing Tony will live there too, so he is thinking of buying it and selling it to Stuart. It's a great location, walking distance to Business is Blooming, and a school and big park with lots of play stations for kids. The problem is that they don't have the kind of money to buy the house. They have a lease at their apartment that they can't break for another few months and they can't afford both. They all have to figure something out."

"Joe couldn't get all this sorted on the phone?" Sarah asked

"He said not. He was really excited about the adoption and loves little Simon so he went down to visit him and congratulate Stuart and Tony in person. He also said he figured Brenda couldn't be so rude to his face as she can be on the phone."

"Why didn't he call you?"

"He said he didn't want to tell me he was going to his ex's and get me thinking something was up."

"That makes no sense to me."

"It makes no sense and perfect sense to me," Charlene said, too weary to figure out what Joe was thinking, just glad he was back and they had a few hours being how they were supposed to be together.

"Oh shoot. I almost forgot to tell you. Joe said there's a way onto the lake from a side road off the highway near the village. A trailer can be backed right into the lake."

"I guess that means Joe could still be a suspect."

"What! Did you talk to Mr. Blake?"

"Yes and he can't account for the whole afternoon. All he can say is that Joe was fixing a motor for some guy, and that it was before lunch but he didn't know if Joe left the shop after that or not. He said he was busy at the front of the house by the dock for the rest of the day and Joe could have gone out. So Joe could have had his motor back and gone out to the lake.

"Anyway, I guess that means anyone could have launched onto the lake without anyone on the lake seeing. I guess the vehicle could be seen from the highway though," Sarah added more to herself it seemed.

Charlene could see Sarah adding that to her mental list of to dos.

"We had a good run at your neighbour across the lake though. He was chatty and we had a good look around his property. We didn't have a warrant but he signed off in Wendy's notebook that he understood he was consenting to us looking at his boats. We thought we hit the jackpot when we saw the blue rope on his boat but It' all intact and looks old and worn so he didn't replace it recently for sure. I think bits of the rope come off every time he ties the boat to his dock, so that's probably what James picked up. He opened up his shed for us and we saw a yellow kayak like yours with the seat out. I think Wendy almost fainted at that point and actually moaned out load when she saw the box of Spider Ultracast Ultimate 10 pound fishing line. Forensics has identified that as the brand of fishing line used to kill Lori. Your neighbour, his name is Bob by the way, said he was making a little cubby hole behind the seat to store his lures. He had a little soft tackle box on the work bench right beside the kayak and he showed us how it fit in perfectly with a plastic hatch he screwed into the top of the kayak so he could close up the tackle bag and keep it dry. He said when he paddled water went down and into the kayak right behind the seat. I've seen you with a damp bum sometimes so I think I got what he meant. He doesn't have those rubber stoppers on his paddle like you do that stops most of the water from running down the paddle into the kayak."

"Was all the fishing line in the box?" Charlene asked.

"He gave us the box of fishing line so we can see if it matches the cut on the fishing line we found on Blueberry Island in the fire pit. That was blood on the fishing line we found on the island by the way, and it was a match to Lori's type of blood, A positive, so not fish blood or something like that. Bob said he cut some line but he cut it in his boat. It was still in his fishing boat and he let us bag it and it looked clean."

"What about the kayak seat? Was it there?"

"Yup. It was in the shed."

"Was he doing a dry run to see if a body could fit inside?" Charlene wondered.

"Maybe. His motor runs rough he said when I asked if I could start it up. He said it skips a bit, and Wendy rolled her eyes at me and opened her mouth. I've got to teach her about poker faces. Something else is interesting though. He said he saw Dan walk up the steps to cottage #2 the day he rented a fishing boat from you. He remembered only seeing the guys on the pontoon boat that morning, so that was the day Lori was killed for sure."

"What was Dan doing there?" Charlene asked, clearly surprised since he didn't say anything like that to her.

"I will go talk to him before I leave here if I can get him alone or get him to come into the station tomorrow. His schedule is for all of them to be in Elliot Lake tomorrow, banging away at rocks somewhere around there, so they have to drive right past the station. The students can hang out at Horton's and wait for him."

"Oh. I have a box of the same fishing line that I gave to Dan when he rented the boat. He said he wound it all back off the reel and got it all back into the box." Charlene got up and opened the filing cabinet and handed the box to Sarah.

"So, you're thinking...."

Charlene could see the confused look on Sarah's face.

"Yes, that's right." Charlene smiled. "I agree with you. If all the line is accounted for Dan didn't kill Lori with any of that line."

"Oh yeah. Good one Staff. I'll measure off Bob's line too."

"Don't forget Greg. He took the same line from the office and put his name on my tab sheet," Charlene reminded her.

"Okay I better get out of here before Joe comes back and you go back into bed."

"What makes you think we were in bed?"

"Are you kidding me?" Sarah walked toward the office door and called back, "Give me a few minutes to see if I can talk to the professor here, okay?"

"Your wish is my command. Besides, I'm adding the boat trip to your tab. Cha ching, cha ching."

CHAPTER 58

Charlene

The rain had stopped and the students and the professor were out on the docks with drinks in hand, in a party mood for the eclipse. Cottagers had the same idea, chairs out on docks. She and Joe waved like royalty from the pontoon boat as she slowly went past them in search of the perfect anchor spot.

The Porters took their fishing boat out onto the lake too and anchored close to one of the small islands, not Blueberry Island, she noticed. She veered away from that island even though Joe suggested it would be a great spot out of view and protected in the small bay. She ignored his request for them to moor there and pretended she couldn't hear him over the motor. She didn't want to go on that island for a long time. She drove the boat onto the shallow waters of a natural sandy beach along the side of an adjacent island where the night sky would be more visible to them, not a lot of trees with boughs overhanging and blocking the view.

Joe got up from the chair and jumped to grab the line to tie off to a tree at the shoreline. He pulled the rope around the branch quickly and effectively. He looked back at Charlene and grinned.

"I love tying knots," he said.

He opened the duffle bag he brought with him from home when he came back. He pulled out the blanket. He moved closer to Charlene and kissed her. She sensed some urgency in his kiss and was unsure what was happening. Was she imagining it? Had it just been a long time since they kissed?

He took her hand and led her to the bench and they sat down. He put his arm around her and pulled her into him and covered them up with the blanket.

"So, Sam told you he saw me on the lake with a woman in my fishing boat towing a yellow kayak and you told Sarah."

Charlene moved to pull back to look at Joe's face, but he held her tight.

"Sam told me what he saw and..."

She could hardly get the words out of her mouth. She wanted to yell that she knew he was not a killer, that she knew she could trust him, that she knew him better than that, but the words stuck. She sat quietly. Her body started to tremble and she knew it wouldn't be long before the tears fell. She realized she didn't trust him fully, and he knew it. But, he didn't tell her he was going to Hamilton or why he was going. He left her wondering why he didn't call and leaving empty air for her to fill with suspicious thoughts. It sounded so stupid in her head. Was that really enough to not trust someone? Not to trust Joe? Did she really love him then? She felt so strongly that she did. She wasn't sure what to think anymore.

"Oh Charlene, Charlene." He got up suddenly from the bench.

The blanket fell to the boat deck. He reached into the duffle bag and Charlene saw the box of fishing line. She could clearly see the logo on the front of the box. Spiderwire. She watched Joe put it into his hands and noticed he had scabs on the top of his hands, scratches that had healed.

Her knees started to shake.

CHAPTER 59

"He said he just went in to check on the girls."

Sarah put out her hands as if to say she had no idea whether to believe the professor or not. She was sitting at her desk with her feet up on her desk, ankles crossed. Officer Edwards was sitting in the desk facing hers. He put his feet up on the desk and stretched out his long legs. He was on night shift and there weren't any calls so he came into the station for a washroom break. He found Sarah sitting and staring.

He took his feet off of the desk after a glare from Sarah.

"This is a privileged position," she said.

"When you write your sergeant's exam and pass it, you can sit like this too."

She knew James made almost as much money as she did with all the overtime and court time he managed to squeeze in, so she wanted some perk for being a detective. Feet on the desk was a small but important thing she thought.

Glad to have a sounding board, Sarah continued.

"He said he walked up the steps to the cottage and knocked on the screen door. No one answered so he called out. He said he was concerned because they both said they were sick. The door from the porch to the cottage was closed so he knocked there too. No one answered so he left and went back into his boat and spent the rest of the day on the water trying to fish but caught nothing, except some great pics of a porcupine on the shore in front of him, which I had to look at and pretend to be impressed and as delighted as he was."

"That proves there was a porcupine," James said.

"No James, it proves he took a picture of a porcupine at a shore somewhere, sometime, and who cares about a porcupine?"

"You could ask him where he was anchored and compare shorelines and check the date and time on the picture," he suggested.

"Not bad Officer Edwards, not a bad idea at all."

Sarah hadn't thought of it and was careful to give credit where due. She needed a good working relationship with all the officers at the station and a pat on the back went a long way.

"I don't think he's a killer anyway," she said. "All the fishing line he got from Staff was back in the box, none missing."

"What about his Ashley theory?"

"No, I don't see that either. The doc said it took someone with great strength to get that fishing line so embedded in Lori's neck and to get her into the kayak and drag the kayak up on shore at the resort and lift it up onto the rack. Have you really looked at Ashley? She's weak. She has zero muscle tone and according to the other students, is a whiner when they have a lot of walking on field trips. I think Ashley played hooky with a hangover and got turned around just as she told us. Her description of the trails she took are pretty accurate according to Staff."

"Why is he trying to pin it on her then?" James asked.

"I'm not sure he's doing that. I think he believes what he thinks about her. It seems the professor was trying it on with her at the campfire and the other students found out. She threatened to report him after the course was over, according to Greg, who got this tidbit from Lori. And Greg said he saw Ashley take a go at Lori in their cottage when Lori told her they all knew she came onto the professor at the Brock pub night. According to all the statements, nobody blamed the professor for thinking he had a reason to put his arm around her the way she acted that night. They seemed more upset with Ashley than their professor."

"Why is she still at the resort then?" James asked knowing he wouldn't be able to figure it out. He could barely figure out Tracy most times.

"Because she had a black out and forgot she came onto him at the pub so when he put his arm around her she freaked. That's what Staff thinks anyway by her reaction when they had a girl chat. Dan didn't figure that out so he is nervous about why she changed her mind and is nice to him now."

"Okay. So Joe? No way would it be Joe," James said as he crossed his arms over his chest ready to do battle for the doc.

"No I don't think so. He comes out of the interview with the Hamilton detective looking so not like a killer."

"He's pretty fit though for a guy his age," James said not

liking what he just said.

"He's pretty fit for any age. Cripes he could run circles around you and me."

Sarah looked down at her stomach. It was flat but getting soft. She better solve this case in a hurry so she can get back to going out for a long walk each day and going to the rec centre gym.

"What about what Sam said? Don't get me wrong, I don't believe it was the doc," James said with more conviction to make up for casting suspicion about Joe.

"Sam said the motor was like the doc's, cutting in and out. That creepy Bob guy has the same motor trouble and I'm sure half of the boats on the lakes around here are old and run rough," Sarah said, knowing Patty had an old motor on her fishing boat that blew out puffs of blue smoke every time it ran.

Patty kept saying it needed expensive parts so was waiting for it to just die on its own. Sarah refused to go out in the boat anyway so it didn't matter to her.

"There's no evidence to say Bob's the killer. Creepiness doesn't really count even though that huge pair of binoculars on his desk bothered me, especially with Staff alone at the resort a lot. His lap top really bothered him though. He kept looking at it and moving it farther out of our reach when Wendy and I were there. He had no scratches on his hands or bruising or anything and Lori fought when she died. He has a limp too remember? There's something wrong with one leg or something. He's out of shape and there's no way he could lift a body and stuff it inside a kayak, never mind lift the kayak and body up on the rack. Did you see his drinking gut? Anyway, when I asked if I could take his computer he said yes. That was a surprise. Phil checked it out and it seems Bob has been blogging and is writing an article for a fishing magazine and has loads of pictures of fish and even more of huge snapping turtles."

"Snapping turtles?" James asked.

"Yup. When pressed about it, he said he's been fishing them and taking pictures and writing about them and included some recipes for turtle meat." she said. "He used Spiderwire 10 pound line to get them."

"That's gross," James said.

"To you yeah, mother earth turtle and all that," Sarah said referring to the importance of turtles as sacred figures to the Native American Indians.

"But," she explained, "lots of people eat turtle and it's an expensive and a highly sought after meat. The MNR guys find snapping turtle as contraband a lot around here fished without a proper licence. Sometimes the meat and turtle bits go all the way to China."

"So he is illegally killing turtles?"

"Yup. Better to admit to that use of the fishing line, than to be a suspect in a murder," Sarah explained. "Besides his fishing line was all accounted for including the piece he cut and left in his fishing boat and we took."

"No porn?" James asked, curious as if that would explain the bad feeling he got about Bob.

"Not unless you include the pics of the turtles on fishing line struggling. Nope, nothing, and he had no chance to delete anything while we were there and he didn't know we were coming and he didn't know we would ask to take his computer."

"Are we going to do something about him?"

"Nope I let the Ministry of Natural Resource people know what he was doing and they will be all over him with probably stiffer penalties than you are I can expect from the courts for our cases."

"What about Greg? He had the same fishing line. The other students said he wanted Lori back. That's a motive," James asked hopefully.

"Yup. That's a great motive. The other guys vouch for him though. He was with them all day until Bob picked them up at the parking lot and took them over to the cottage where they worked on their assignment and had a few beers at the picnic table."

"So who does that leave us with?"

"Nobody," Sarah said. "We got nobody."

CHAPTER 60

Monday September 28th, 2015

"Hi Sam," Dan said as he and Haiden and Ashley got out of Jack's fishing boat at the parking lot.

"What's up?" Sam asked

"Jack is giving us a hand by getting us over here. Charlie didn't answer the office doorbell. The pontoon boat is docked in the usual place at the resort and her fishing boat is there," Dan said pointing over to the dock beside the one Jack was holding onto as Dan and the others got out of the boat.

"Peter and Greg are in the van already. Jack brought us over in shifts. It's not like her to not be ready," Dan added.

Smiling at Jack, he thanked him for helping them and walked to the van and drove off.

"I can take you over Sam," Jack offered.

"Hmm? Yeah okay," he answered. That was not like Charlie for sure. He looked back at the parking lot. Charlie's car was there. The Porter's car was there and no others now that the students' van was gone.

"Maybe she had a late night watching the eclipse with that

friend of hers. We were all up really late doing the same thing," Jack said as he put the motor into reverse and backed away from the landing.

"What friend?" Sam asked.

"A man with a Scottish accent. I haven't met him, but we heard them talking on the pontoon boat last night as they were heading out on the lake to watch the eclipse."

"Okay," Sam said.

Maybe not okay, he thought.

CHAPTER 61

"You look rough detective," Officer Fisher said as he looked at Sarah. "Are you still wearing the same clothes I saw you in all week-end?"

"No I am not wearing the same clothes."

Sarah looked down at herself as she stood by her desk sorting through clear plastic forensic bags. She didn't remember wearing the same shoes yesterday.

"Not all the same clothes anyway. What are you doing here looking so fresh and chipper on your day off?" she asked him.

"I left some stuff in my locker. That terrible week-end of driving the boat around in the sunshine, mostly sunshine, chatting with nice people, looking at the fall colours, must have made me delirious and I left my sunglasses and wallet here when I finished my shift. Yes I drove here without my licence, no I won't do it again. I promise," he said and gave her his charming smile.

It had no effect on Sarah and he laughed as she just stared at him.

"What are you doing?" he asked picking up a bag. "What's all this?"

"Cripes Allan! Murder investigation! Young woman at Staff's place! It's evidence. Don't tell me you didn't know!"

"Yeah, yeah I heard it on the news and there was chatter in the locker room but I was away for two weeks on holidays. I just got back for the last shifts," Allan said defensively.

"What's with the blue rope? Was she tied up with that or something?" he asked.

"Oh Christ Allan. You need to get up to speed. You need to know what's happening. You're my eyes and ears out there for God's sake." Sarah grabbed the bag from him.

"Yes her hands were tied up with it and we found this blue rope tied around a tree at the shore where we're certain she was killed. Some bits of fishing line were in a fire pit stained with blood, Lori's blood type. There were blood stains on the rock beside the fire pit too, also Lori's blood type."

Sarah pointed to the other evidence bags.

"Poor kid struggled. We got lots of skin and blood from under her nails. She must have really scratched her killer up. She scratched at her own neck and chin trying to get a finger hold to stop him from choking her but she's got more than her own DNA under her nails for sure."

"Sarah..." Allan started to say something to her, but stopped and just stared at her.

"What?"

"This is probably stupid," Office Fisher said.

"Whenever someone says 'this is probably stupid' it usually isn't. Spit it out."

"I don't know. I stopped a guy in a fishing boat to check his licences etc. He had the same blue rope hanging from the bow of his boat. It looked like it was used to tie an anchor, only there was no anchor and the rope wasn't long enough to be of any use to tie off to a dock. It was pretty useless really. I asked him what happened to it but I don't think he really answered me. He had a rock attached at the stern to marine rope as an anchor. I was just interested in basic emergency equipment."

He looked at Sarah and she was staring at him not moving. He continued, sure it was going to be stupid but thought he may as well carry on since he was almost finished, and the way Sarah was staring at him was making him nervous.

"He was messing with fishing line that was all tangled in his tackle box while I was checking out his boat operator and fishing licence. The backs of his hands were covered in scratches. I guessed that he hooked himself a few times while he was trying to untangle the line while in the tackle box. He had a mess of hooks in the box. The boat was a mess too and the motor was about to conk out when he put in in gear. I remember thinking he may not be out fishing too long and was glad he was close to the launch. He had paddles so I left him alone."

"What was his name Allan?" Sarah asked moving closer to him.

"He was a big friendly guy."

"Name Allan?" she asked quietly, holding her breath.

"He joked about going to the Black Cat for wings, not beer, or something like that anyway."

"Name Allan! Name for fuck sakes!" Sarah yelled at him.

CHAPTER 62

Charlene

Joe dropped Charlene off at the landing and turned around and drove away to get back to the police station to talk to Sarah. She knew she was late, but a group of angry students and the professor were the least of her worries. That she and Joe had an argument last night was way down the list of what was important right now too. Sure he saw the look of fear on her face when he reached into the duffle bag and shuffled around until he brought out the container with the upside-down apple cake he made just for her and the plates and forks.

"Don't worry Charlene, there's whipped cream to go on top," he said laughing when he saw her face as he pulled out the cake.

His laughter died when he realized she was seriously frightened and the argument started when she told him why she was. Argument was not really a good description of what happened, Charlene thought. There were few words spoken. The feelings and emotions were loud enough. Of course he was hurt that she didn't trust him and thought he was a killer.

He did seem to listen to how she came to that conclusion though, and of course the fishing line would be in that duffle bag. It was the one he had by the door of the shed to grab quickly and take for the truck or the fishing boat. He told her he was in a hurry to come back to her to spend the night with her but forgot to bring the cake and a warmer jacket. He just grabbed the closest bag, his utility duffle bag.

He also told her she would never have thought he could kill anyone if she trusted him and really knew him. Of course he was right. Being right was not what Joe wanted. He wanted to be wrong. He wanted Charlene to know him right down to his core to trust him with anything. The tears flowed, and not just hers.

After they calmed down Joe told her he wanted to surprise her by just going to her house and not anything more than that. No hidden agenda. He didn't want to upset her by telling her about his ex. He said he just wanted to go to Hamilton and back quickly and deal with it and not worry her. He told her he loved her but didn't think she loved him. How could she, he said, if she thought he was going to kill her? She told him she did love him but she could feel a twinge of her own doubt even as she said it.

Joe told her he was working on a motor the day Lori was killed and didn't leave his shop so he wasn't out in his boat on the lake with Lori or anyone. He said he let the guy use his own motor and he didn't bring it back until early evening, so he didn't even have a motor if he wanted to go out on the lake and kill somebody.

He said Stuart's cat was under a bushy plant with large

leaves and woke up scratching him when he was helping Stuart and Tony move things around in the flower shop.

When she asked him if the Hamilton detective or Sarah asked him what the guy's name was, he told her no one asked and if they did, he wouldn't have known it at the time. He didn't get his name when he first came in, he just had a phone number. He shrugged off the look on Charlene's face that told him she didn't like his book keeping.

"What do you mean the first time?" Charlene asked.

"He came in again on Saturday just after I got back, to see if his motor was fixed. I have a part on order so it's not ready. I got his name then and put it with the phone number. He wanted to go fishing so I let him use my motor again. He still has it."

Charlene told him what she was thinking and they took the pontoon boat back to the resort to call Sarah. It went to her voice message.

Charlene and Joe took her fishing boat to the landing to go to Joe's shop to get the guy's name. She thought if she left the pontoon boat, Dan could take the students over in the morning in case she wasn't back yet. She didn't realize until she arrived and saw the students' van gone, that she forgot to leave a note for Dan taped to the office door. Well, she thought, they got to the van somehow. Sam maybe? How did Sam get over though? Shit. What a mess of a day she thought. Going to the shop, driving to the police station with the name to give to Sarah, up all night talking to Joe and no chance of the day getting any better. Sure, she thought, now she was certain Joe was no killer. It's too late now. What the heck had she been thinking? Of course Joe was no killer. She was sure the guy who had Joe's motor was the killer at the start of all this. Of course it was that guy! What else would explain Sam saying it was Joe's motor? It WAS Joe's motor! Why did she have to go and doubt Joe? It was because she didn't trust him. She didn't really trust anyone anymore she realized, feeling sick to her stomach.

CHAPTER 63

Charlene

"Good morning Sam," she said as she opened the door to the office and found Sam on his knees stoking up the wood stove.

"Hey Charlie," he said as he stood up and walked toward the door.

With a slightly visible drop of his shoulders and what Charlene thought she heard as a sigh of relief, Sam left the office.

Charlene saw the Porters' boat was gone so figured they wouldn't be in the office for anything. She went upstairs and put the coffee on. It was another beautiful sunny fall day. The nuthatches were busy working their way down the big pine tree in front. The red squirrels were running and chattering and scolding her for being late for the students and late with her trust. She noticed more hostas in the garden in front of the office were missing leaves. The deer must have been grazing again. That's the end of buying any more hostas. What's the point anyway? she thought. She may as well sell up and move away. She couldn't bear to live so close to Joe and not be with him.

"We got him!" Sarah said as Charlene picked up the phone.

She had come down to the office to check for e-mails while the coffee was perking and the phone rang making her jump. Man she was tired.

"Is Joe there?" she asked.

"You heard me right Staff? We got him!"

"Yeah. Sorry. I'm glad Sarah. It's a good thing we left you that name."

"What? What name? When?"

"Last night, early this morning, whenever we were there."

"You were here?"

"Maybe we should start again," Charlene said too weary to carry on like that.

"Joe and I went to his shop and got the name of that guy who borrowed Joe's motor and we took it to the station and left it with the guy at the front counter for you. We think he's the killer."

"Wait a sec."

Charlene could hear Sarah yelling in the background. Oh oh. Someone's in trouble she thought.

"Here it is, the note I was supposed to have in my hand the second I walked in here. Well, what do you know? He's our guy and he's sitting in the cell down the hall."

"You just got the note and you have him in a cell? You are one amazing detective Sarah."

"Yup, thank God, or that dude working the front desk would be looking for another job," Sarah said. "Officer Allan Fisher had a hunch and it paid off. He remembered the name of a guy he talked to a few days ago while out checking licences on one of the lakes just off the highway. He remembered cut blue rope and scratches on the guys hands and a mess of tangled fishing line. Nothing seemed suspicious at the time but when he saw the same stuff in evidence bags on my desk, something twigged. We went to go talk to the guy and when he opened the door, the guy just said, "You got me. Yeah I killed her." He got his coat and walked out to the cruiser. It was unbelievable. We brought him back here and he's been talking ever since."

"It's the guy who borrowed Joe's motor right?"

"Right. He said he got onto the lake at that launch by the highway, that dirt road, the one you told me about. He picked up Lori and took her to the island and killed her."

"Whoa! Details please and hold on a sec. I have to go up and turn down the coffee." Charlene set the phone down and ran up the stairs.

"I'm back. What's the connection to Lori? Did he know her? Why her?"

"I was going to ask him about Lori's glasses so I left the interview room and checked my cell for the picture of Lori wearing her glasses so I could have the picture up while I asked him about them. Sure enough, he's the guy at the bar standing beside Lori in the picture. The students told me Lori was really happy the night before she was killed because she was really hitting it off with someone at the pub. Him. That's how he met her. They arranged for him to come to the resort the next day to go for a boat ride and picnic. He said Lori really wanted to try kayaking the way Greg kept talking about it, so they took your kayak and towed it to the picnic spot.

You were in the back bush working so they figured you wouldn't notice.

"He said she wouldn't let him touch her when he tried it on with her so he decided to kill her. He said he wasn't planning it. He just used what he had on hand. He was putting the fishing line on his reel as they were sitting by the fire pit getting ready to catch their picnic. Once he killed her he cut the blue rope that was attached to his boat and anchor, the one you found tied to the tree. He said he never took chances and made sure his boat was tied off properly. He said he knew how the winds could change. Cripes! The winds have changed for him for sure. He cut the rope and just left his anchor in the lake. I have to remember to send someone out there to go back and look for that."

There was silence on the phone line while Charlene imagined Sarah making a note to herself.

"He tied Lori's hands up with the blue rope he cut and put her in the kayak and towed the kayak back with Lori stuffed in it. He put the kayak on the rack hoping we'd think it was Greg. Lori told him about Greg and how everyone knew he was trying to get her back. When I asked why he put the kayak on the rack the way he did, he said he didn't want the birds to get to her. So, he's a considerate bastard. Anyway, then he just took his boat back to his truck and went home." Sarah could hear Charlene trying to interrupt but ignored her. "Yes, yes, we're getting the details, I'm just giving you the short version."

"What about Lori's glasses?"

"Oh yeah. He heard it on the radio about the glasses being

found and sent some local chick to your place to say they were hers."

"What reason did he give her?"

"He said he didn't. He said she has a huge thing for him so he took advantage of her feelings and she didn't ask why. We have the glasses. The forensic guys are there now. We were able to get a warrant authorized a couple of hours ago and the glasses were sitting on his nightstand beside his bed, obviously the side where he sleeps. Don't ask how we know that for sure. Disgusting is all I can say. He's given us a DNA sample, even though we had lots to choose from around his house. Yuck! Wendy had to type out the warrant and we got that too, even though he was willing to consent. We're sure the skin and blood from under Lori's nails will match his. He said it would."

"He's too creepy Sarah," Charlene said feeling chills down her back. "Has he said he's killed before? He's too chatty."

"Yeah we're going to have to pull the missing persons file and have a go at him. I asked him and he just smiled. He's talking a blue streak about Lori, but saying nothing else about anybody else."

"What a huge relief Sarah. Oh man," Charlene said feeling herself deflate with the news.

"Oh man is right. I am so relieved. I didn't know where to turn. It's crazy how it ends like this. An officer not even up to speed on what was happening, a hunch, and a "You got me." It's amazing how boring and normal it all seems."

Charlene knew the feeling. She worked cases where the suspect talked and talked and pleaded guilty when it came to trial and the justice process just flowed along. It seemed weird that would happen, but it did. She was glad for Sarah. The case was really wearing her down.

"You can't have your kayak back. I forgot it would be evidence. How I almost forgot that I don't know. The sheer size of it maybe? Anyway it will be too cold to kayak soon. You should get it back in a few years," Sarah laughed. "Besides, when Phil pulled your kayak seat out from under one of the blueberry bushes on the island, it was in a few pieces. The back support was snapped and the side pieces looked like they had been just ripped from the kayak. Just think though, you could shop for a new one after you tally up what we owe you for transport and the cottage rental for Ashley etc. That should be a hefty cheque."

"What does the guy do for a living?" Charlene asked, curious as always about the kind of person who kills another, but also not wanting to think about her kayak and what she was going to do.

"He's a bricklayer out of work right now. Strong hands and big build."

"Mr. Blake said he lifted the motor off of Joe's boat and put it on the dock without much effort," Charlene said.

"I can see him doing that. He won't be lifting anything but prison weights for a long time," Sarah said.

"I gotta go Staff. Thanks for everything. I'll talk to you later."

CHAPTER 64

Charlene

Charlene puttered around the office tidying up the fishing lures and sweatshirts and tee shirts. For some reason, guests really like the sweatshirts she had for sale and some guests bought a new one each year. They were made somewhere in Manitoba and had a beautiful feel to the fleece and the colours were vivid with Kirk Lake Camp in small stitching over a stitched design of a moose or fish or bear. The price tag was vivid too and each year she thought she'd have a big inventory left over but she didn't. There weren't any adult shirts left. She pulled the kid shirts out and folded them and put them back on the shelf in order of size. A few adult tee shirts were balled up and on the wrong shelf. She thought she should probably count what was left against the order sheet, but didn't want to know really how many were stolen when she wasn't in the office. She didn't really care. That was for them to care she thought, folding them up.

The students were still out on some rock somewhere, the Porters out in the fishing boat somewhere, and Sam was doing clean-up on the property just outside the office window where he could see her. She smiled. He was checking up on her. Oh, there are good people, she thought, and it made her heart feel a little lighter. Too bad she would have to let one of the best ones go.

She moved to the office counter to set her coffee down. It looked like it needed a good cleaning. She saw some money on the counter, the exact amount for the fishing line. Joe's name was crossed off the tab sheet and signed off as paid. He must have done that the night before when she went upstairs to the bathroom before they drove to his shop to get the name of the guy who killed Lori. All debts paid between them.

The unexpected ring of the landing phone startled her.

"Hello?" she asked.

There was a lengthy pause before she heard, "Goodbye Charlene."

Time stood still.

"Goodbye Joe," she replied.

Charlene put the phone down and picked up her binoculars. She walked out of the office and looked across the lake. Joe was standing at the end of the dock looking back at her. They stood there, divided by water and emotion, for as long as it took. Charlene lowered the binoculars.

With a twirl of tartan, Joe turned and walked to his truck and drove away.

###

ABOUT THE AUTHOR

K.L. McCluskey graduated from Print Journalism and wrote freelance for almost 40 years before she started writing her first book, A Kayak for One. Her writing included a weekly fitness column, full length feature stories and a stint as a reporter covering court and town council meetings.

Overlapping the writing years, she was a police officer with Hamilton Police Service and worked in patrol, the Criminal Investigative Department, and the Special Investigation Branch as a detective in the Sexual Assault Unit. By the time she left her policing career she had attained the rank of Acting Staff Sergeant. She then bought a 12 cottage resort in northern Ontario. Six years later she sold the resort and taught Police Foundations at a college in Sudbury, Ontario until she moved to Victoria, B.C. for a short time. She moved back to northern Ontario, also for a short time, and now lives in a small eastern shore community in Nova Scotia.

She enjoys her time travelling to visit her daughters and grandchildren, and while at home enjoys writing, kayaking, hiking, biking, and exploring the beauty of the east coast.

THE KIRK LAKE CAMP SERIES

Book 1: A Kayak for One
Book 2: Two Buckets of Berries
Book 3: Three for Pumpkin Pie?

Coming soon.

Book 4: Fore! In the Hole
Book 5: Cocktails at Five
Book 6: Six is the Limit

Made in the USA
San Bernardino, CA
27 September 2018